Credits:

Edited by Mollie Traver

Cover Design by Deranged Doctor Design

ALEX LIDELL

LERA

LUNOS

OF

POWER OF FIVE BOOK 4

ALSO BY ALEX LIDELL

New Adult Fantasy Romance

POWER OF FIVE (Reverse Harem Fantasy)

POWER OF FIVE

MISTAKE OF MAGIC

TRIAL OF THREE

LERA OF LUNOS

Young Adult Fantasy Novels

TIDES

FIRST COMMAND (Prequel Novella)

AIR AND ASH

WAR AND WIND

SEA AND SAND

SCOUT

TRACING SHADOWS

UNRAVELING DARKNESS

TILDOR

THE CADET OF TILDOR

~

SIGN UP FOR NEW RELEASE NOTIFICATIONS at
https://links.alexlidell.com/News

1

LERA

This is a bad idea. I step forward, struggling to tune out my own warning.

The sunbathing tiger gives a sleepy snort, his orange- and black-striped body completely covering the fountain's stone bench. Eyes closed, the great cat has his head pillowed on one large paw, the other front limb hanging lazily down to the ground. Whiskers as long as my forearm sway in the breeze, and the twitching of the cat's closed eyes speaks of exciting dreams.

However dangerous provoking a sleeping tiger might be, the alternative—letting Tye's animal form continue to lie in the middle of the Citadel's courtyard—is worse still. With the rising sun now bringing trainees and staff outdoors, someone is going to get hurt. Killed. Unlike most shifters, Tye's tiger is unaware of his fae self, which makes him as dangerous as the wild animal whose form he takes.

I take another step forward, my heart pounding. If River is willing to throw King Griorgi off his throne for the sake of

Slait and Lunos, then evicting Tye from the Citadel's central fountain is the least I can do. And then I'll make the bastard tell me why he shifted in the first place.

I extend my knuckles toward his wet nose, the three paces between us too far for touch but too close to save me if the tiger pounces. *A very, very, very bad idea.*

"Good morning there, Tye." I keep my voice low and steady, trying to slow my racing heart. There is nothing more appetizing to a predator than fear. "I know you *are* Tye. And you know me too, don't you? You are Tye and I am Lera, and you are not going to maul me."

The morning mist has burned off, leaving golden autumn sunlight, whispering red maples, and a crisp square of green grass and white marble spreading away from us in each direction. Sparrows whistle back and forth, hidden in the branches overhead. Stunning perfection—perfection that Tye's tiger is daring to mar.

"If it were up to me, I'd string the trainee to a whipping post for this stunt," a male says behind me. One of the Citadel guards—a pair of them appeared a few minutes ago, their eyes searing my back. With their standard-issue forest-green uniforms and air of jaded boredom, they stand out easily from quint trainees. "The male knows full well that his damn beast is rabid."

"How long has it been here?" The second male's voice is low, more likely to avoid attracting Tye's attention than to conceal itself from me.

"Half the damn night. And now it looks like its breakfast is here."

"I've two darts," Guard Two says. "Want me to shoot its ass?"

I spin toward the two males, my eyes flashing. If River

were here, he'd likely have some appropriately diplomatic way of sending these two to hell, but the prince is scheming with Autumn in the library as he's been every minute of the three days since discovering Griorgi in Karnish. So the bloody guards will get me instead of diplomacy.

Power surges inside me, saturating my muscles. Not magic —I have no magic without echoing one of my males. But sheer, utter fury is a power of its own. "Hurt Tye's tiger and I will tear your throats out."

I little care how much smaller I am just now. How mortal. If one of them picks up that crossbow hanging on his belt, they will both have me to reckon with.

And then they can explain to the council why they killed Klarissa's pet weaver.

The guards exchange a look and take a step back, their hands rising slightly to show no intention of reaching for a weapon.

I turn back to Tye.

"If she is too stupid to live, that's her problem," one mutters to his partner, who snorts in agreement.

Right. They have me there.

I step toward the tiger. Still sleeping without a care in the world, oblivious to the havoc he is wreaking in the Citadel's courtyard.

"What do you say to napping elsewhere?" I murmur, aware that we are drawing more and more attention. Warriors in training. Visiting scholars. Staff. All gathering for a show, muttering condemnations of an out-of-control shifter. As if Tye is some spectacle to be gossiped about. I take another step toward him. "Your kitty form is . . . Well, the Citadel guards are running out of clean underwear."

The tiger gives a small feline snort, his top lip curling up to show fangs glistening in the sun. I wonder if that's a yes or a no. If I'm the reason Tye has taken this form to begin with. In the days since the trial—or maybe even before then—the emerald-eyed male has grown more distant. Skipping meals. Avoiding eye contact. And now this. *Why? Talk to me, Tye.*

My soul strains for a connection with him, its absence like a tiny, persistent nail being driven into my flesh. I want more of Tye, but he . . . I don't know what he wants. Just that it isn't me. Maybe that's why some part of me is insisting on doing this myself instead of calling for River or Coal, a part that's desperate enough to hope Tye's tiger might acknowledge me. Might convince his fae counterpart to grant me a chance.

Still snoozing in the sun, the tiger looks like a giant orange plush toy, or perhaps an overgrown housecat. *A housecat in whose world you are a mouse.*

I take another step toward him, nice and easy, trying to quell the urgency in my stomach. "Could I share your bench?"

One eye opens, emerald green with an elongated pupil, and regards me lazily. The tiger is blissfully unaware of anything but the stone bench beneath him, the sun on his fur. There is no Emperor Jawrar in his world, no coiled tension of River working out a plan to dethrone his father, no vulnerable human wielding more magic than she can control. I wonder what it might be like to wake up in the morning to discover your limbs aching from a hunt you don't remember, your belly full of meat.

Someone curses behind me and I realize the little scene is gathering an outright audience. I even hear a bet exchanged and cringe with the certainty that good money is not on me.

The tiger closes both eyes, having apparently decided me not worth bothering with. Certainly not when something as important as a nap is at stake.

"Bloody stars, one of you stop that insane idiot," a voice full of command bellows across the square. From the sudden commotion around me, I take the approaching male to be the captain of the Citadel Guard, and I curse to myself. But I don't dare break focus to turn toward him. The voice gets closer. "Mark my words—if that mortal gets hurt on your watch, there will be more blood soaking this grass than you bastards would like. Same if I so much as smell a gaming ledger."

The two guardsmen from earlier suddenly bracket me, one approaching from each side, their eyes narrowed, teeth bared in resentful anger. "You heard the captain." The one on the right spits on the ground beside my foot. "Step. Back. You mortal idiot."

Wonderful.

"You've my gratitude for your concern, guardsmen, but the tiger is my quint mate," I say, summoning a calm, respectful tone on the off chance that I might still talk myself out of a confrontation. "I accept full responsibility for whatever happens."

The spitter snorts. "Like your *accepting responsibility* will mend any of our hides." His leering gaze slithers over me as he cracks his knuckles. Dark, cruel eyes linger on my breasts, where my nipples have peaked in the morning chill and show too plainly through my burgundy tunic.

I step back, my heart stuttering.

Spitter lunges for me, his fingers digging painfully into my shoulders. A full head taller than I am and stout as a wine cask, the male smells of acrid sweat and the eggs he ate for breakfast. Lowering his voice so only I can make out the words, he whispers into my ear, "Whatever reason the magic chose you, it wasn't for brains, wench. If you like it rough—"

5

That is as far as he gets before the tiger, sleeping peacefully a moment ago, suddenly launches himself at the pair of us.

I feel the impact of the animal's shoulders as he hits my hips, knocking into me so forcefully that I fly backwards. My breath leaves me as I land hard on the ground.

A pace away, Spitter screams, his voice wet and ear-piercingly high, as four parallel gashes bloom across his chest. Bright-red blood soaks his green uniform and the tips of Tye's claws.

Setting all four paws on the ground, the tiger surveys the grass: Spitter, down and bleeding; the second guard—and everyone else—wisely backing away; one mortal female on the ground, trying to scoot back.

The tiger's attention pauses on me and I freeze as the animal circles. Stops. Yawns. A white muzzle cocks to the side, green eyes full of familiar condescension meeting mine.

Fear dries my mouth, making the sides of my vision waver to blackness. The sun feels too bright, the wind too cold. My muscles tighten, ready to run, even as I can't bring myself to look away from the approaching predator. Beneath me, the damp grass soaks through my pants in cold spots.

The tiger follows as I inch away. Stalking one step for every foot I move. Probably enjoying the damn game, contemplating whether human meat would be to his delicate liking.

He opens his maw, showing a full set of glistening teeth. When I shudder, he lifts a massive paw into the air, the same one that left Spitter in tatters.

The sight of blood still clinging to those sharp nails shoves all rational thought from my mind. Before I can stop myself, I lunge to my feet and *sprint*. My boots pound the ground, sinking into the soft earth. Warriors, trees, buildings, everything but the path forward blurs in my vision. I think of nothing but my steps. *One. Two. Three. Fo—*

The tiger tackles me from behind, flattening me to the ground. Air leaves my lungs again as I fall, the smell of grass and cat filling my nose. I brace for the pain, the sting of slashed flesh.

A large, warm weight settles atop me instead. Seven hundred pounds of feline pinning me to the earth, thick fur covering my face.

Squirming toward oxygen, my head emerges from what I realize is the tiger's armpit. The weight atop me shifts ever so slightly and settles again. Heavy. Relaxed. Then the tiger opens his mouth and brushes his wide, rough tongue over my ear.

Again. And again.

An insane chuckle escapes my tight throat. Then another, before a string of deranged giggling—the kind that can only be evoked by the absurdity of a bath from a killer tiger—rushes from my chest. "That tickles," I say, twisting my face. "That—"

Click.

The soft sound sends ice down my spine. I see it a moment later—Spitter loading a crossbow with a barb-tipped arrow. Taking aim. His partner doing the same.

"No!" I bellow into the morning air. "Don't shoot! For stars' sake, don't shoot."

"You're as rabid as that thing," Spitter says—and pulls the trigger.

2

LERA

A flash of light blinds me, a rush of power filling my veins as the tiger atop me shifts into Tye's fae form. A hissing heat singes the air above my head. A fraction of a heartbeat later, two hunks of deformed metal thump to the ground. Barbed crossbow bolts melted in the nick of time by Tye's flex-honed magic.

Whispers ruffle across the grass-covered square, the voices breathless, disbelieving.

"Impossible. Bloody impossible."

". . . melted a half dozen in the practice arena—you should have been there."

"That's . . . Do you remember Tyelor of Blaze?"

Ignoring the whispers, Tye rises from where his body covers mine, the dark pants and wine-colored tunic he wore when he shifted once more hanging loose on his muscled frame. His red hair is streaked with sweat and his green eyes are chilled enough to be Coal's. The silver earring that usually makes him look carefree and cocky now just makes him look menacing. Heartbeats pass while his eyes focus, recognition finally flashing in them.

"Tye—" I start.

"Approaching my tiger was inexcusably dangerous, Leralynn," Tye says quietly, stepping between me and the crowd.

My stomach sinks, hurt squeezing my ribs.

Spitter, one hand pressed against his bleeding chest while the other still clutches the crossbow, blanches. "Now you listen here, *trainee*—"

"Those were barbed arrows, not sleeping darts." Tye's voice is ice. "And there was a human in their path."

Spitter's partner, who fired the second bolt and now stares wide-eyed at the melted remains of it, retreats a step. "We were protecting the Citadel." His voice rises, claiming justice. "You are the one who put the girl in danger. Who put all of us—"

Tye's hand flicks and thin collars of white fire encircle both shooters' necks, a finger's width away from their skin. "You thought my *tiger* was the more dangerous of us?" His voice has hardened from ice to steel.

The guards' throats bob, the crowd around us drawing a collective breath.

"It's Tye, is it not?" The captain of the Citadel Guard, whose voice I heard earlier, steps forward through the sea of parting spectators. A distinguished, dark-haired male with gray at his temples, the captain has his hands in his pockets, his shoulders straight but easy. "Some unfortunate choices have been made this morning. Let's not make the list any longer than it must be."

"Get River," Tye says coldly. "I'd like my quint commander present. Library, west wing."

The captain snaps his fingers, sending an underling off at a trot. "Done. Meanwhile, I'd be obliged if you would release my guardsmen. One of them is injured, as you can see."

"Your guardsmen are fortunate to be alive at all," Tye replies, the tension in his voice and back squeezing my chest. I've never seen the quick-to-smile male like this before. Neither, I wager, has anyone else at the Citadel.

Taking a step forward, I gently lay a hand on Tye's arm, the coiled muscles beneath his burgundy shirt as hard as chiseled stone. His jaw clenches. "Tye?" I say gently. "Look at me."

"I am holding a very delicate piece of magic just now, lass," he answers without turning his head. "As magic and body are connected, it would be best if you withdrew your hand lest I accidentally slip."

I remove my hand, my stomach sinking even further. Despite standing close enough to feel the heat of Tye's body brushing mine, to smell his fresh citrus-and-pine scent, I've never felt so far away from the male.

"What's going on?" By the time River's voice sounds a few minutes later, the guards in Tye's hold are trembling outright. My own nerves fray at the ends as well. Hands behind his back, River strides up to stand beside the captain of the guard, his gray eyes taking in everything around him without effort. His towering height, cropped brown hair, and tailored blue jacket make my heart stutter in relief—and make every guard in this square look like a ragtag child.

Silence pulses. My ears ring.

"Leralynn?" I realize River has asked me a question. Of everyone's here, mine is the first assessment he wants to hear. *When did that happen?*

"Tye's tiger slashed one of the guards after said guard

11

grabbed my shoulders," I say, aware of the many eyes boring into me. "The same guardsman and his partner then fired barbed crossbow bolts at Tye. Tye melted the arrows before they could strike and . . . restrained the guardsmen pending your arrival."

"The tiger was holding Lera when the bastards fired," Tye says with barely restrained fury. "If those bolts had connected . . . Call for the final trial, River. I want to be free of this place."

"Tye," River starts quietly. "We're all still recovering from Karnish. Leralynn's training is—"

"Lera has trained enough."

Leralynn's training. Besides Griorgi's whereabouts, it's all anyone has talked about. Any moment I haven't been eating or sleeping—or sneaking away for a moment of solitude, as I was when I found Tye's tiger—I've been in the practice arena with some combination of Coal, Tye, Shade, and Klarissa, trying to weave together multiple threads of power without blowing up the whole Citadel.

The captain of the guard clears his throat, keeping his eyes on our commander. "If I am not mistaken, River, my guardsman only grabbed your female to keep her out of harm's way. And while they used a poor choice of projectile, they only fired after the *trainee* assaulted one of them. The penalty for a trainee's assault on a guardsman—"

"Flog my male for assault and I'll execute yours for attempted murder." The nonchalance in River's voice reverberates through the square. He turns slowly and, being the largest male in the gathering, looks down at the captain of the guard. "Play the intimidation games with someone else, sir. My quint is out of your league."

The captain thinks for a moment then nods reluctantly.

River looks at me for a moment, an apology in his beautiful gray eyes, then turns to Tye. "I will request the final trial for tomorrow. It's the best I can do."

"Fine." Tye flicks his hand again and the collars of fire around the guardsmen's necks disappear. The two males fall to their knees as Tye turns on his heels and strides away.

Standing beside River, I watch Tye's departing back, a chill seeping into my bones. "It's my fault," I whisper. "I wanted to understand why he'd shifted, and I rushed in head on. If I hadn't tried to move the tiger myself, if I'd listened to the guards, if . . . Stars, River, if you want to yell at me, I don't think I'd mind. Maybe I'd even feel better for it."

Taking my shoulders, River turns me to face him, his earthy scent filling my nose. Despite my worry, my belly tightens when I look up into his storm-filled eyes, high cheekbones, and strong jaw. He's so handsome it hurts.

"Stars take me," River whispers after a moment, drawing me against him. My face presses into his hard shoulder as he rests his head atop my hair. "You've no notion of how fortunate we are that this ended with only a few gashes."

"That doesn't sound much like yelling." I try for humor but my voice trembles as images of could-have-beens fill my thoughts. "Aren't you furious?"

"I am." River's arms tighten around me, pulling me closer. "At myself, not you. I've never seen Tye so angry, Leralynn— never even imagined seeing him so close to losing control. Coal, yes, but not Tye. It's my job to know when one of my own stands on a cliff's edge, and I missed it. I . . . I'm worried. I can't even tell you why Tye's tiger was in the middle of the square to begin with. That isn't like him."

I tilt my head away, studying River's face. Around us, the group is dispersing, the captain of the Citadel Guard clearing away both his males and the spectators with a veteran's proficiency until it's only River and I left by the burbling fountain.

River rubs his eyes with the heels of his hands.

"It's okay, River." I pull his hands down and hold them tightly in mine. "You've had a few things on your mind." The weight of responsibility that River carries on his shoulders makes my heart ache. "Working out a way to save Lunos from your father and Emperor Jawrar, for starters. Even you can't be everywhere at once."

"That isn't an excuse. Whatever this is, whatever's happening with Tye, I can't take him into battle this way." River exhales, shaking his head.

"He'd tear you limb from limb if he heard you say that, you know," I murmur softly, the pit in my stomach growing heavier.

"Your faith in my self-defense skills leaves something to be desired." River presses his forehead to mine then runs his lips softly down my cheek, ending at my jaw. A trail of heat follows in its wake. "Come. If we're leaving here as quickly as it appears we need to, we've some planning to do."

"Right." I force a smile onto my face. "The small matter of staging a coup. We better get to it—the Slait throne won't seize itself."

3

RIVER

*R*iver surveyed his quint, all finally gathered in the suite's common room. Despite Leralynn's attempts to locate Tye, the male had stayed away until just a moment ago, when he strolled in wearing that mask of familiar cockiness. As if he hadn't come within a hair's breadth of killing two guards that morning. As if the shift into a wild predator in a place that could get him put down for it was no more serious than a pilfered bottle of wine.

Just another of the many petty crimes River had tried for centuries to punish out of the male, all without bothering to discover why Tye did any of it in the first place. Three hundred years of fighting together, of living together, weathering triumphs and sorrows, and it wasn't until now that River glimpsed the demons lying in ambush behind Tye's easygoing demeanor.

Something that seemed to have taken Leralynn, on the other hand, only a handful of weeks.

River wondered whether the girl had any notion of the

power she had over them. How deeply she opened their souls. How bloody frightening it was.

Pushing all thoughts of Leralynn firmly to the back of his mind, River waited for Tye to find a seat. Instead of his usual spot on the couch—and as close to Leralynn as possible—the male took a chair for himself, balancing it precariously on its hind legs. Ensuring that no one could come near. In addition to the five of them and Autumn, Kora was in the room too, standing with her hip braced on the couch's far armrest.

The female warrior's dark brown hair was in its usual cropped style, one emerald stud glinting in her ear. Now that Kora's quint had passed all their trials and were free to do as they wished—and go where they wished, which seemed to be never far from Autumn—River noticed that Kora's air of confidence and command grew stronger by the day. She wore a finely tailored black tunic with pale green trim, leather pants that showed off her leanly muscled legs, and a thin silver chain around her neck that disappeared below her shirt collar. River would bet money it was a gift from Autumn—an expensive one, if Kora's nervous toying with it was any indication.

"I understand that by this time tomorrow, we'll be done with our remaining trial and on our way from the Citadel," Shade said. Snatching up Leralynn mid-step—and in the middle of braiding her hair—the wolf shifter pulled her onto his lap with an ease that made River's cock twitch in jealousy. Her thick auburn hair spilled over her chest, making her brown eyes narrow in exasperation. Shade leaned back against the cushions, snuggling the girl firmly against his bare chest. "What happens next? We go after Griorgi?"

With the smell of a fight filling the air, Shade fell into his role as River's second with practiced ease. Clear, calm, ready to enforce orders.

"Almost." River nodded to him. "Regarding the trial, yes, it will be tomorrow. It was Tye's request to expedite it, but we can't stay here much longer anyway, not with Griorgi advancing his plans with Mors. As for going after him and Jawrar—that is a bit more complex."

"We don't know where they are, do we?" Leralynn asked.

River frowned at the vulnerable curl of her shoulders, the tightening around her eyes. "No," he said carefully, watching her. All of a sudden, she seemed a million miles away. Despite the ongoing conversation, the need to discover what was happening in that gorgeous head of hers hit River like a thunderstorm, rousing every protective instinct inside him. And while he was exploring her head, he wouldn't mind discovering more of her body too. With everything going on, it'd been three days since their coupling after the Karnish battle—which was three days too long.

Bloody, burning stars. They were speaking of battling Jawrar and dethroning Griorgi, and here River's mind was plummeting into his suddenly too-tight trousers. His cock hadn't roused this impertinently since River was a colt. He cleared his throat. "Autumn's people report that he's not been in Slait since escaping Karnish. Autumn and I have tapped every resource at our disposal to find him, but"—he looked at Autumn, who burrowed deeper into her iridescent silver wrap —"our father is slippery."

Leralynn flinched, covering the reflex quickly.

"I believe Jawrar is back in Mors, at least," Autumn said, reclaiming River's attention. "If he stepped into the Subgloom when Karnish collapsed, which must be how he disappeared so quickly"—Autumn looked to Kora for confirmation before continuing—"then he'll only be able to exit in Mors. Unlike the Gloom, the Subgloom is strictly Mors's territory, which, with our wards, makes it a one-way passage no matter where you enter it. This means he must now wait for Griorgi to open a new portal before he can return to Lunos."

"Should we go hunting?" Coal asked from his customary place against the wall by the door—just in case anyone should come barging in to murder them.

"No." River stood to relieve the pressure that his trousers were putting on his enlarging groin. "I little want to walk us into whatever stronghold he has set up, whether it's elsewhere in Lunos or in Mors itself. We'll draw him to us instead, make him come to the Slait palace."

"He'll have to come home eventually," Autumn added. "And come alone—Griorgi is too smart to build a portal inviting qoru directly into Slait."

"Griorgi isn't the only one who'll be alone," Kora said, slipping her arm around Autumn's shoulders. "The Citadel won't be able to send quints into Slait to assist you."

River nodded then, catching Leralynn's confused look, turned to explain. "The Citadel can't assist in dethroning a king without destabilizing the whole realm. Blaze and Flurry would believe themselves vulnerable to similar tactics, and before long we'd have everyone protecting themselves from the Citadel instead of focusing on Mors."

"Plus, overt aggression would give Griorgi the support he needs to rally an army," Autumn said, pulling her silver-blond braids up into a high bun as if preparing for battle this moment. "Slait subjects would take up arms to defend their homes. Keeping it a family affair means fewer deaths all around."

"Speaking of fewer deaths," River said, deftly picking up Autumn's words even as he braced himself for a storm. "You truly do need to remain in the Citadel, Autumn."

"No," she said immediately, her sharp gray eyes daring River to take this line of conversation any further.

River crossed his arms over his chest. For all her brilliance, his sister could be as foolish as a colt. "Stop and think. If I fail—"

"Oh, shut up." Autumn waved a slender hand at him. "I've been trying to see it from your point of view, I truly have, River. But I can't get my head quite that far up my ass."

River's blood heated, shooting through his veins. Jaw clenched, he squared off against his sister, who flicked a bare toe at him, one delicate silver ring flashing on it.

"Unless you've hidden another magic mythos scholar up your sleeve," she said, before he could so much as utter a sound, "you are going to need my expertise. Or did you imagine some scenario where you and Father drag a pair of clubs into the throne room and take turns bashing each other on the head? Granted, I don't know who'd win that." She added the last part under her breath.

Kora was up and between them before River's hand could close around those damn braids. "Perhaps I might offer an alternative solution, Prince River?" the blue-eyed female said, holding up her hands. "If the prince of Slait might *invite* my quint into Slait Court, we would be happy to provide a protection detail for his sister. I believe such an arrangement would be subtle enough to avoid seeming like Citadel interference."

"Bodyguards following me around like nursemaids?" Autumn's fury turned on Kora. "No."

"The arrangement would have some fringe benefits," Kora murmured, running a knuckle along Autumn's flushed cheek —which, ridiculously, just made River long to do the same to Leralynn. Further proof of how hopelessly distracted he was.

19

Autumn scowled despite leaning into Kora's touch like a cat. "The answer is still no."

What leash remained on River's control broke with a resounding *snap*. His balls ached, his quint mates were brewing secrets, and now Autumn was digging her heels in just to be bloody contrary. After what Griorgi did to their mother, Autumn's balking at so light a precaution was one step too far. River's top lip curled up to display his canines. "You incorrectly presumed there was a question somewhere in there."

Autumn's face darkened. "You wouldn't."

"Wouldn't what? Pull rank and *enforce* that order?" River's jaw clenched. Blood rushed to his head, the heat of it burning his ears. When he spoke, his voice was so low and dangerous that the males exchanged cautious looks. "You want to test me? Because I don't think you'll enjoy the results."

"Test you?" Autumn slid to the floor, her hands curling into fists as she glared up at him. "Do you imagine for one bloody second that—"

"Stop it." Leralynn's voice cut through the air, seizing River's chest. Climbing to her feet, the mortal put her hands on her hips and glared at River, her eyes liquid fire. River actually took a step back from the force of them. Even Tye lowered his gaze from its survey of the ceiling long enough to glance at her in surprise. "Whatever enforcement you are about to threaten is not going to go over well. Especially for you, River." Leralynn's hair whipped behind her as she twisted to Autumn. "As for you, is keeping Kora away just to make a point to River really worth it?" She shook her head. "Maybe instead of arguing about how best to pack for Slait, we can focus on tomorrow's trial and getting the hell out of the Citadel. I, for one, have been here long enough."

The stunned silence of the room wrapped itself around Leralynn. Glaring at each of them in turn, the female turned on her heels and marched to her bedchamber, her too-large uniform tunic billowing around her small frame. "Call me when the stupidity wears off," she called over her shoulder before slamming her door shut.

"Does anyone know what the bloody hell happened to our mortal?" Coal asked, arching a brow at the resounding thud. "Because I like it."

4

LERA

I slam my palms against the windowsill, grinding my teeth. Removing Griorgi from power is the one vital thing that must be done to ensure Lunos's future—and we've no notion of where the bastard is. Why? Because when we had Griorgi in our sights, I lost control of the echoed magic and let him escape. And now we have a greater mess on our hands than we did before.

"Leralynn."

I flinch at the sound of my name in the hallway. The door opens and closes behind me as I look out the window. Beyond the glass, the dense forest surrounding the Citadel grounds ripples and flutters with unseen life, white clouds scurrying overhead in the autumn breeze. Everything is so intensely green and red and orange, the grass and plants drinking in the Citadel's magic. Even the damn foliage has more control than I do.

Behind me, River clears his throat. "Were you challenging

Shade for the role of second back there?" he asks mildly. "Or me for the whole quint?"

When I turn, the sight of the sculpted giant's piercing gray eyes, taut abdomen, and corded arms crossed over a hard chest sends a shiver from my spine to my thighs. His face is a study in smooth strength and intoxicating control.

Stars take me. I know he is the same male who I snapped at a few minutes ago, but that was outside. In the common area. Here in my bedchamber, it is too difficult to wall off my memories of our other activities, when River's skillful command of my body turned my bones to liquid and had my senses exploding with pleasure.

I wrap my arms around myself and meet River's eyes, my chin up. "If you've come to remind me that you are the prince of Slait or quint commander, or to—"

River takes a step forward, grasping my hips. "I don't recall you minding the commander too much a few days ago," he murmurs into my ear, his soft, rumbling voice making my skin blaze so hot it's a wonder the drapery doesn't catch on fire. River chuckles before reining in his voice. "But actually, I came to tell you that what you said in the common room was right on point."

"I—wait, what?"

"Autumn and I have a tendency to squabble." He shrugs. "Shade says he keeps waiting for us to grow out of it but is losing hope by the decade."

"So you weren't really going to . . . I'm not sure what you were going to threaten actually."

"I'm not fully sure either." A corner of River's mouth twitches. "But it would have been very firm. And about as useful as Autumn protesting a protection detail. We'd have worked out as much eventually—you just sped up the process." The humor fades from his too-perceptive eyes. "What I want to know now is what truly set you off back there."

Besides that one small detail of my having let the greatest menace known to Lunos get away? Not a thing. "I . . ." I rub my face, debating the best approach to this.

River's firm fingers cup my chin, tilting my face up to meet his. The male's strength and sense of responsibility engulf me much more potently than they did before our coupling three days ago. Who knew that sharing a bed with the male—truly sharing—would send my body and soul into as much of a tailspin as it did my magic. "I'd appreciate the truth, please, Leralynn," he says. "Given that you expect as much from me, it does seem fair, no?"

The fight leaves me much faster than it has any right to, and I know I will give him the answer, even as I glare. Stars. Those piercing gray eyes might hold more magic than just earthquakes. "Why is yelling at you in the common room so much easier than holding my ground in private?" I mutter.

River smiles, his flashing white teeth confusing my senses even more. Still holding my chin, he rubs his thumb over my mouth. "Because the bedroom and the battlefield are two places I never yield," he says and, without waiting for an invitation, presses his lips over mine. *Takes* a kiss. Deep and thorough and so sex-clenchingly strong that my underthings dampen.

He pulls away, his nostrils flaring with satisfaction. Smelling my arousal.

My skin heats.

With a small chuckle, River sits on the edge of my bed, the tall mattress perfect for his height. Opening his knees, he pulls me to stand between them, our eyes nearly level. His broad hands brush along my shoulders, my hips, the undercurve of my bottom.

My breath catches at the memory of what he did *there* when we last lay together, my face flaming hot enough to melt metal. I hated it. My treacherous body, however . . . My thighs clench and I try to step back, only to find myself trapped in the male's muscular arms.

"It's time to answer my question, Leralynn," River says, his silver-speckled eyes holding mine. "No evasions, no half truths. I love you. Which means I need to know what had you curling in on yourself back there. What truly set you off?"

Stars, how closely was River watching me to see my body shift? Before I can push the thought away, the memories that sparked that reaction return to wash over me mercilessly.

We were together, River and Coal and Shade and Tye and me, my body echoing the males' power. Holding enough of it to stop Griorgi and Jawrar. Except I didn't. I brought the whole damn town down around our ears instead. If River, so injured he could only crawl, hadn't gotten to me in time to take control of the magic, we'd all be dead. "I'm the reason Griorgi is free," I manage to say finally. "Because I couldn't control the magic. And now everyone is paying for it."

River studies me, his broad shoulders filling my vision, his thoughts too deep to read.

"*And* we have our final trial tomorrow, with no more do-overs," I blurt out. "We're one more crazy Lera explosion away from being put to death, whether by my hand or the arena's wards."

Still, River stays quiet. Watching. Listening.

I squirm to back away, but he lifts me to sit sideways on his lap instead. "Settle down, Leralynn," he says into my ear. "And then listen to what you just said. My father has tainted Lunos for nearly a thousand years, managed to break the ancient wards that hundreds of thousands of fae and mortals died to erect, and allied himself with Mors's emperor. And yet it is you whom we should hold responsible for the mayhem?"

I shake my head. River is missing the point. "We had him in Karnish. If I hadn't—"

"Griorgi had *us* in Karnish." River's voice hardens. "And if you hadn't connected the quint, we'd be dead."

"I—"

"You failed to singlehandedly defeat the king of Slait, yes. I heard you the first time." River shifts me to have a full view of my face. Those deep, beautiful eyes study me with disconcerting intensity, as if nothing else exists in the world. With his formal jacket shrugged off somewhere in the common room, the heat of his body seeps through his simple white shirt, filling the air between us. River brushes a knuckle down my cheek. "And I told you that you saved our lives. I wouldn't like to have to repeat myself again, luv."

Luv? Heat. Sheer, burning heat engulfs my skin, starting from the spot along my cheekbone that the male just touched and shooting straight through my core. My blood and sex heat at the same time, the indignation and flash of fury as strong as the sudden grip of excitement. The former emotion wins, and I shove River's chest. "Bastard."

He captures my wrist, his large hand wrapping easily around my forearm. "Unfortunately not." His deep, masculine voice brushes my neck. "I fear my lineage is something everyone is quite certain of."

My thighs tighten, suddenly very aware of being atop River's. The bed, the dim bedchamber, the low voice . . . the unyielding gaze and grip that the male has on me. I squirm beneath the pressure of his attention, only to discover a

27

decided hardness beneath my bottom. With the next heartbeat, I can't bring myself to care about the king of Slait or the emperor of Mors or the trials.

River's gray eyes spark, raw desire flashing through the mask of control. His lips part, taking small gasps of air as the hardness beneath me pulses gently. Beneath his crisp, tailored shirt, his muscles coil so hard I feel the tiny vibrations of his rippling tension. "Leralynn . . . " He swallows and the arm he has around me releases to grip the edge of the mattress in a white-knuckle grip. "There are a great many things going on just now. I don't imagine you want . . . You better leave the room. Not too quickly, please."

My gaze narrows, the very notion of denial rallying my body into alert. If I'm the prey the fae warrior's instincts sense me to be, I'm a bloody willing one. "It's *my* bedchamber." My voice rings through the heated air. Free of River's restraining arm—which my body wants back where it belongs, no matter what my logic whispers—I twist until I'm facing the male, straddling his thighs as if riding a horse. "You don't get to order me out of it."

My hand goes around his neck, my heart pounding as I pull his mouth down toward mine.

A growl vibrates River's chest, his hand tangling in my hair, tilting my head roughly to the angle he desires. When his mouth takes mine, the deep, possessive warmth of it shoots heat all the way to my slicking sex. The clenching intensity of sensation floods my senses and I jerk back. *Try* to jerk back. River's grip on my hair tightens, keeping me in place as his unyielding kiss deepens, his tongue claiming my mouth.

A fresh jolt of flames sears my nerves, tightening my muscles all the way down to my curling toes. Stars, the male hasn't even touched me down low and my body is already approaching the edge, desperate for more. It's one part infuriating to three parts intoxicating.

From beyond the door, voices rise and fall in conversation, the echoes of Shade's sensual laugh kindling flames of a different sort. Shade. Tye. The others, just beyond the door.

River pulls back at once, studying me until I want to squirm again beneath his intense scrutiny. "What's wrong, luv?" he asks. *That* word again.

"Nothing." I sound breathless, my swollen lips slow to obey.

Hand still twined in my hair, River tips my face up toward him. "Tell me." An order.

Instead of kicking him for it, my treacherous body shudders with desire. "The others. They, well . . . They are all very close just now. En masse. I—I can feel their magic more than I used to." After our explosive connection in Karnish, their threads, their essences, are impossible to ignore. It almost feels like we're all in this room together.

A hint of amusement colors River's gaze. One hand still in my hair, his other slides down my body, a slow growl of appreciation accompanying its journey between my heavy breasts, down my belly, and into the waist of my trousers. With an immortal's maddening patience, he runs his fingers through my wet folds. "The others likely have worked out what we are doing by now." He raises his now glistening fingers and inhales my scent, before cocking a brow at me. "Did you want them to watch?"

My eyes widen, my heart hammering against my ribs. "You wouldn't."

River chuckles. "I'd forgotten for a moment how much more . . . closed mortals are about such things. Fae are more visceral." He licks my wetness off his fingers. "One day perhaps."

"No," I say forcefully. My sex throbs.

River gives me a look that sees all too much. "In that case, you may wish to keep your voice in check." His own lowers. "A feat that I intend to make very, *very* difficult."

5

LERA

I draw a short, sharp gasp as River tosses a pillow onto the dresser top. Lifting me up, he bends me over it, my toes just touching the floor. A heartbeat later, his hands expertly relieve me of my trousers, leaving my upturned backside open to the nippy autumn air, my sex open to *him*.

Pulses of need rake my sex and shoot down the backs of my legs. I squirm to release the tension between my thighs, to stop the already growing ache, but River places a strong hand on my lower back and presses me down.

His other callused palm massages my backside, waking each nerve to his touch. "You are beautiful," he murmurs, leaning down to whisper into my ear, his hardness pressing against me. "And just now, you are at the perfect height for me."

My breath hitches. My sex tightens, my hips undulating in spite of myself. "Stop talking," I say between clenched teeth.

River chuckles again, the rich sound so unusual from him that my bones sing.

His voice changes suddenly, taking on that air of command that my mind resists but my body goes crazy for. "Open for me, Leralynn," he orders, his hands already on my wet, quivering legs. Pushing them apart until I can't clench at all, my aching insides utterly dependent on him for fulfillment. My knees try to close on instinct, but River's thighs are there. Blocking me. Holding me in place. Letting me feel the restraint. "Settle down."

I take a breath. Release it. Will my muscles to loosen.

"Very good," River says softly, moving his fingers to massage the lower curve of my backside before sliding along my aching sex. Forward and back, forward and back, the wet sounds and my unsteady breaths filling the quiet room, each stroke ending maddeningly shy of my apex.

With a shudder, I arch up toward him, receiving a teasing flick of my bud that makes me gasp. A thick trickle of wetness slithers down my leg.

River catches it, wipes it away with his hand, and—

"No!" I tense, trying to squeeze my backside together even as the male pulls apart my cheeks. The last time he went near there . . . Stars. I've never hated and loved something so much at the same damn moment. Have never felt a release as strong as when he . . . filled me so thoroughly. The thought of it, of him—my heart races.

"I'd keep my voice down if I were you," River says softly, his free hand returning to stroke my wet folds. Circling my opening. Teasing my swollen bud with soft flicks. Right. Left. Right. "Unless you've changed your mind about that audience, of course."

I grip the sides of the dresser, barely biting back a moan. Each of River's ruthless caresses sends a fresh wave of need coursing through my blood. The sensation is so strong it hurts.

Aches. Screams. Sweat beads along my temples, my body trembling from the approaching abyss. When the tip of River's callused finger scrapes the hood of my apex, I shudder violently. One more stroke and—

He stops.

I whimper.

River's other hand, so patiently waiting on my bottom, brushes between my cheeks. "Open."

I shake my head.

Another circle around my opening, my wetness smeared along my bud until I writhe with need. Close. So, so close.

"Please," I beg, my body convulsing against the restraints. Needing the release he teases. "It hurts. I can't. I need—"

River taps my bottom, and this time, I've nothing left with which to resist. With firm insistence, he traces the entry, slicking it with my own desire. "One day it will be me in here," he whispers, sliding his finger into me. In and out. In a bit further. Out. In further still. The stretch and burn of it merges with the pulsing in my sex until I can't tell the difference between pain and pleasure.

River's weight shifts as he frees himself, the hard tip of his shaft positioning itself at the edge of my sex. With a twirl of his finger that triggers every nerve inside me, he thrusts, sheathing himself to the hilt.

The double fullness magnifies each thrust of River's cock, its wide head playing along my ridges. *Thrust. Thrust. Thrust.* The dresser creaks under his force, and I push back against him, making River growl and move faster. The male pulses inside me, my own swollen apex throbbing in rhythm. When his hand returns to caress my bud one more time, I no longer care who hears my scream as I tumble over the edge.

"Stars," River grunts, timing his own release to follow

mine. His warmth spills inside me, a harmony to the aftershocks still raking my flesh. A few heartbeats later, his strong arms gather me against him. Sitting on the bed, he pulls me onto his lap, stroking me gently. "You are beautiful when you climax," he murmurs into my ear. "Just listening to you find your pleasure makes me find mine."

I smile in sleepy contentment against his hard chest.

The chest moves.

Blinking, I realize River has laid me flat on the bed while he pulls off his shirt and wraps the material around the bedpost. "What are you doing?" I ask.

He grins. "Only getting started. Now, give me your wrists."

THE FOLLOWING MORNING, the glow from River's intense attention yields to nauseating anxiety as the five of us fill the preparation room. The now familiar scents of leather and salve, sweat and sword polish, fill my nose. Outside the windowless space, I know hordes of Citadel warriors-in-training are climbing to the top of the bowl-shaped arena, readying to watch the morning spectacle.

In their defense, every one of our bloody trials has been a spectacle.

Even now, before the gong has sounded, we are already an exotic anomaly—a quint with runes from the second and third trials already wiped, preparing to repeat the first challenge they once forfeited.

My loose, wine-colored uniform hangs off my body, revealing my bound chest—the last time I'll ever have to wear the oversized tunic, stars willing. Vaguely, I feel my males moving about me, tightening armor and choosing weapons and waiting around with that annoying nonchalance that I can't seem to master.

A knock at the door jolts me from my thoughts, and my brow knits at the sight of Klarissa, her dark hair and champagne robes rippling in the low light.

"Please forgive the intrusion." The female's melodic voice brushes right past me to wrap like a silk scarf around River. When the male raises his gray eyes to her, Klarissa smiles, holding up a folded note that makes my stomach clench with dread. "After some deliberation, the Elders Council has decided to add a small condition to your trial. I'm certain you will see the wisdom of the council's decision once you think on it."

"Will I?" River's voice is hard enough to crack stone.

"Of course." Klarissa uses her long, painted fingernail to perfect the parchment's folded crease and hands the message to the prince. "After all, at the end of the day, it is truly the weaver whose power must be demonstrated. If you yourself will not trust Leralynn in the safety of the arena, how can the Elders Council trust her in the wild? That is simply not a risk we're willing to take."

Klarissa is gone before River can shake open the letter, his jaw tightening once he does. "The Elders Council has instructed that our weaver is to take charge of the magical movements during the trial." River folds the paper carefully, all his attention on the task for several heartbeats before finally sliding up to meet my gaze. "Furthermore, the council would like the weaver to be the one who retrieves the flag."

"What?" Stopping in the middle of the preparation room, I stare at the commander. After the destruction I wreaked in Karnish, no sane person would let me anywhere near the males' power. And for all her viciousness, Klarissa isn't daft. "She can't be serious."

"She can, and she is." River runs a hand through his hair, his back straight. "The rest of us may assist, but the primary magic is to come from you, Leralynn."

Silence settles into the air, slowly seeping into my bones. Before I can find my tongue again, a large body comes up behind me, bringing the smell of wolf and rain. "You'll be all right, cub," Shade murmurs into my ear, his heavy arms resting on my shoulders. "I promise."

"Me?" My hands ball into fists, my blood heating. I step away from Shade and turn on the male. On all of them. "It's not me I'm worried about. Our surrenders are used up. If we fail to retrieve the flag this round, the wards will kill all of you. This isn't the time for me to be playing with my new toys, and River needs to go to Klarissa and make that clear."

"I don't believe I can," River says with a gentle apology.

"Good." Coal's voice snaps like a whip, cleaving the room's nervous energy. Leaving off the sword buckle he'd been adjusting, Coal uncurls to his full height. Dressed in his usual black leather pants and vest—a silent defiance against the maroon uniform shirts and sashes that the rest of us wear—and low blond bun, the male's hard face holds an edge of steel. "Because Klarissa is right."

"What?" I twist fully toward him.

"The battle in Karnish shook you, mortal." He crosses his arms. "Hiding from your power beneath a fuzzy blanket isn't doing you—or anyone—any favors."

"Are you insane?" For a moment, I truly mean the question. "I can face my bloody fears in a practice arena, when your life doesn't hang on my staying in control."

"Practice arena?" Coal's eyes blaze. "How has that been

working out these past few days? Because I've seen no more progress from you than from that punching bag over there."

"That's enough," Shade growls, flashing his teeth at the male.

"No, it isn't." The restrained violence in Coal's lithe muscles sings loudly enough to fill the room. "There is not enough stress in the practice arena to truly make her understand her power. We have tried that already—we've tried everything. The council is, for once, bloody right—it *is* time for a change. Time for her to stop hiding from the colossal power she carries within." Coal turns to me, his eyes blue flames. "Because when we leave here, mortal, the stakes will be higher than losing our lives in a trial."

Blood pounds in my head. "You want to lecture me on facing fears?" I advance on the male, my fingers curling into fists. "Let's start with how you've barely touched me since—"

"Enough." River steps between Coal and me, his heavy hand settling on my shoulder. "You are both right, and it doesn't matter. Coal's motivational strategy aside, the council wasn't making a suggestion, Leralynn. When that gong rings, you will need to take the lead."

"Fine." I raise my chin, moving out of River's reach as I swallow the bile creeping up my throat. "The council wants me to go after the flag, I'll go after the flag. You lot can stay as far away from me as you wish. Better yet, as far away as possible." I rub my face, the reality of it finally sinking in, replacing the fury—if not the fear. "The fewer of you I need to worry about maiming, the better."

"We aren't going to abandon you, cub," Shade says, turning me to face him. With his long black hair tied back, the lantern light plays over the strong angle of his jaw and gives his yellow eyes a golden tinge. His thumb traces my cheekbone and brushes lightly over my lips. "We are your pack, and we're trusting you to lead us in the trial. You are a warrior in your own right, now. You just need to see it to believe it."

The warmth of Shade's words spreads over me. Pack. Yes. We are a pack, and the strength of that knowledge slows my pounding heart. Before I can say as much, Shade grips my hips and lifts me into the air until my face is inches from his own.

"But you *are* going to be careful, cub," he adds in a low voice, the command filled with enough power to send it pulsing down my spine. His nostrils flare delicately, taking in my scent, while his masculinity whirls around me, saturating my senses.

I start to nod my agreement, freezing when Shade's eyes flash with a predator's hunger. With a wolf-quick snap, his teeth catch my lower lip, the canines forceful enough to draw tiny beads of blood. When my mouth opens with a gasp, Shade seals his lips over mine. His tongue invades my mouth, claiming me with strokes that are nothing short of possession. None of the other males dare approach while Shade marks me thus. While I kiss him in return.

The wolf might keep his mating instinct well under control most of the time now, but the pack knows when to give him space. Just as they knew to give River and me our time last night. A warmth spreads through me, the connection of all five of us cocooning my soul.

"I love you," I whisper when Shade returns me to the ground, my gaze sharing the words among them all. Even Coal. "I love you."

Shade growls his agreement. Coal nods, his eyes blazing into mine. River lets a corner of his mouth rise with pleasure.

When my attention turns to Tye, the redheaded male stretches lazily.

"Of course you do, Lilac Girl," he drawls. "Who wouldn't?"

Before I can respond, the arena gong echoes through the room. Shade shifts in a flash of light, making my breath catch in my throat. Then two hundred pounds of lethal wolf presses against my thigh, keeping me company to the slowly opening arena door.

Our final trial has begun.

6

LERA

*S*and, great dunes of it, shimmer in the sun. The desert stretches around us on all sides, filling my vision. I know the vastness is an illusion of the arena's wards—the same wards that keep the spectators above from entering the arena or hearing what's said within—but the sensation of being in another place altogether is nonetheless disconcerting.

The arena's magical sun bakes the earth, us, everything in sight. It's hot—hotter than I've ever felt it before, though I might just be imagining it. The heat is an equalizer, making sure we're all uncomfortable and all motivated to win and get out of here. Sweat springs from my temples within moments.

"Is that wee Viper's quint over there?" Tye says, holding a hand over his eyes and jerking his chin toward the other side of the arena. He bends to secure our team's wine-red flag to his belt. "They're a decent lot of males. Nothing like Malikai's."

Without the fae's preternatural senses, all I see is a group of five warriors in matching sky-blue tunics. The smallest of the five mirrors Tye in fastening the flag to his clothing. *Smallest*—even the tiniest of fae warriors outweighs me by half. I lick my dry mouth. "Does Viper turn into a Viper?"

"No," Coal growls. "Pay attention, mortal. It's your magic, not Viper's, that we're here to test."

Putting a hand on my shoulder, River turns me away from Coal. "The objective is simple: Obtain possession of the other team's flag and bring it back here." Calm, easy words. "Where is the flag?"

"Viper has it."

"Correct. So I want you to use your magic to isolate Viper from the others. We are going to add the cords of power one at a time. Go as slow as you need. Do you understand?"

No. My heart hammers, banging against my chest. "And once I isolate Viper?"

"Once you isolate Viper, the rest of us will hold back his quint mates while you take the flag." The calm confidence in River's voice is both supportive and terrifying.

"But—" I cut off at a flash of Coal's eyes. Glancing back at Tye, I find our own flag on his belt, waving like a kill-me-now target. The burgundy cloth clashes with Tye's mess of red hair. If all goes according to plan, the male will stay back and out of the way, protect the flag, and leave the fighting to us. To me.

Tye grins. "I cower helplessly behind your slender back, oh Great Protector."

"You have teeth, claws, and several hundred pounds of deadly muscles the moment you want them, kitty cat."

A shadow passes over Tye's face, almost too fleeting to see. "Very true." His quick smile and light voice churn my heart. "But it still sounded good."

Before I can reply, River takes my hand, his magic

immediately rousing an echo inside me. The force of his power is so strong that I stagger as my body wakens to it. The phantom limb of magic, utterly absent moments ago, now uncurls like a bear stomping along the ground. *Ba-bum. Ba-bum. Ba—*

"Easy, Leralynn," River murmurs, beckoning for the others to join us. The males connect to me slowly, feeding me their power as gently as they can manage. Nonetheless, when all four cords of magic light up inside me, the sudden tsunami of magical force takes my breath away. My heart pounds. My lungs stretch. The energy inside me roars an untamed fury strong enough to eclipse the sun.

Strong enough to rip me to shreds.

Across the arena, Viper's quint is busy drawing something on the sand. The blue-clad warriors may be our assigned opponents, but I know that our true enemy is the one blazing inside my chest.

"Easy," River repeats, his voice firm but soothingly low. "The power obeys you, not the other way around. You are a weaver. Feel each stream of magic."

I draw a shaky breath and do as River says, focusing my awareness on one cord at a time. River's earthy power is dark brown, heavy, strong, with all the delicacy of a grizzly bear. Tye's feline fire is hot, orange impertinence. The silver of Shade's healing power carries a wolf's need for connection, for rounding and protecting a pack. I use it to wrap around the first two, combining the squirming brown and orange cords into a single broad rope. And then there is Coal.

The last male's power is unlike the others. All those years as a Mors slave turned Coal's magic inward, its purple cord splitting into hairs that work their way everywhere. Filling my muscles, waking my nerves, spiking my senses until each grain of sand seems its own stone. The thin purple strands spread through everything and hold on tight.

The thick weave of silver, brown, and orange cords whips violently in my hold, but Coal's purple strands reinforce my body. Make me strong enough to withstand the pressure of the others.

This feels new. A slight improvement over any time I've wielded the magic before. I let cautious hope fill my lungs. Maybe Coal was right to agree with the council—maybe now, in the arena, will be the moment I take true control.

"I'm all right," I tell River, my voice shaking only slightly. "You can let go. I no longer need the direct contact to reflect your magic."

Obediently, River pulls his hand out of mine and draws the dulled sword strapped to his waist. On my left, Coal does the same, pulling a sword off his back. They begin to pull away in either direction, forming into a short line across the sand. Shade's wolf gives me a forlorn look then lopes to the other side of River.

A rush of panic makes my throat close as I realize I am on my own, no River to take control of the power if things go badly.

"You've not destroyed the arena or the sun quite yet," Coal calls dryly, one blond eyebrow quirked, as if reading my thoughts. "A better start than I expected."

I give him a vulgar gesture, though my heartbeat slows.

He tosses me his sword, drawing the spare blade he has sheathed down his spine for himself.

"Seriously?" I call, splitting my attention between the weapon suddenly in my hand and the coil of magic flailing in my preternatural weave. "I'm not sure I need another means of destruction just now, Coal."

44

"No, but trying to kill someone can soothe the nerves." He hefts his spare blade into a better grip. "Try it yourself against Viper."

Looking across the sand, I see that Viper has conveniently separated from his quint, the other males fanning into a line behind him. Seeking me out, Viper sets a course in my direction. The blue flag waving from his belt is plainly bait, but I have my own game to play and this works well enough for my purposes. As he gets closer, our eyes meet across the sand and Viper smirks, though the crooked smile holds more mischief than malice. His quint mates move more slowly behind him, aiming for my males.

I glance compulsively back at Tye, who's pulling at a thread on his uniform sleeve with a bored expression.

"Mortal," Coal snaps, his patience with me plainly wavering. "River, Shade, and I will try and protect the wee red-haired princess while you go play with Viper. Get a move on."

Fine.

Gripping my blade tighter, I walk toward Viper, who's growing larger in the shimmering heat. His grin widens. Up close, his smaller stature gives way to a wall of lean, ropy muscle. He has sharp features, a constellation of freckles, pale red hair, and blue-green eyes. The sword in his hands might be dull, but the steel still gleams in the arena's sunlight. *Not alone*, I tell myself, my mouth dry as Viper and I enter weapons range. *Not alone. Not alone.*

Viper's blade swings for my head, the blow clean. Crisp. Skull-shatteringly strong.

I snap my sword to parry the blow, Coal's power surging through my muscles. The blades meet with a deafening clash, the force of which rattles my bones.

45

Viper kicks me away, his boot sinking painfully into my belly.

I fall backwards, desperately gulping air. It's all I can do to roll over my shoulder and scramble to my feet before Viper's blade impales the sand where I lay a moment earlier.

The dry heat is sapping my energy faster than I'm used to in training.

Stars. Aiming the tip of my sword at Viper's heart, I lower my level until my thighs roar, and lunge.

Viper sidesteps from my line of attack, his sword swinging in a powerful arc. The blade whistles through the air, the light reflecting off it making me squint. My heart stutters, my breath clogging in my lungs. I twist on instinct. Angle my blade down. Meet the blow with the center of my steel.

"Someone's been training with Coal," Viper says, a note of approval in his voice, like a spark of light in the darkness. A moment later, his voice drops, his accent—an echo of Tye's, with its songlike syllables and strong, rolling r's—hardening. "You'll need more than that to get my tail, lass."

Viper strikes again, moving as fast as his namesake, the *whoosh, whoosh, whoosh* of his sword assaulting without a moment's pause. I block each strike, my muscles screaming between the blows. Each collision forces me back, one step at a time.

Strike, block. Strike, block. The escalating attack drives me into a never-ending retreat. Sweat snakes down my face, stinging my eyes, while rising bits of sand coat my panting tongue. The sound of my own rasping breath is harsh against Viper's soft grunts, the ringing of clashing steel.

Strike, block. Strike, block. No end. Never an end.

Distantly, I notice action at the edges of my vision. Bodies in combat as my quint fends off the other warriors, the clang of metal so steady that I know my males aren't playing to win, but to buy me time.

And Viper isn't playing to win either. He's playing for a different reason. My eyes widen as I spin from another blow. "You . . . are . . . herding me." My words come in gasps.

"Aye." Viper grins.

"Where?"

"Och, to just about . . . here." Before I can scream, the male snaps his fingers and a shield of shimmering, opaque silver encircles the two of us in a space twenty paces across and at least fifteen smooth, impenetrable feet high. A wall of magic cutting me off from my quint. The burnt sky overhead only intensifies the feeling of being caged.

"What the bloody hell is that?" With my sword between myself and Viper, I rush to the shimmering wall and find it solid as stone. "River!" I bellow with all the air left in my lungs.

River, River, River, the echo calls.

"They can't hear us." The self-satisfaction in Viper's voice burns through me. "It's a static shield. It exists on its own now, without us needing to hold it. Took all our magics and a great deal of study."

I reach desperately for the connection to my males—and find silence. Even my sense of Coal is gone, cut off from me by that shield. There will be no additional magic to echo, but my existing weave of power, that thick braid of silver, brown, and orange cords, still whips about, purple wisps magnifying its force. A great weave of a quint's full power, all within me, and no way to get to River for relief. No safety valve. No one to help rein in the feral monster that I've woven into existence.

Cut off. Alone. Isolated.

My vision darkens at the edges, wiping away my fatigue.

My muscles tighten. My lungs expand, each fiber in my body trembling with energy even as the storm of panic bubbles in my veins. Out. I need out of here. Now.

I slam my fist into the shield, my knuckles screaming at the impact. Nothing. Again. Pain erupts in my bones, and I stare at the blood now leaking from my hand.

The braided magic inside me flails, slipping from my grip.

The earth underneath us gives an ominous shake. I scramble to re-grasp the magic, nausea from the effort rising in my stomach.

"Stop," Viper shouts, the amusement gone from his voice. "I won't touch you. The shield will—"

My ears start to ring, cutting off sound. The cords of magic slip further, even as I dig my nails into them. My sword thumps to the sand, my breath halting, all my concentration going toward holding on while the magic rears like a terrified stallion.

With the next jerk, the thick weave pulls free of my grasp and lashes like a whip against the shield.

Hits. Bounces. Ricochets into the ground.

The earth trembles, portions of the ground rising up and down like waves. Again. Again. Each shocking quake greater than the last. Up and up, before falling from beneath our feet.

"What are you doing?" Viper bellows. "Stop! For stars' sake, stop."

"I can't!" I snatch desperately for the bolting beast, only to find it wilder still, vengeful for the earlier restraints that led it into this trap. Determined to shatter that opaque shield jailing us here.

The wounded earth quakes again, rising in a wave so massive that it launches me into the air.

Viper throws himself at me, twisting to take the brunt of

the impact as we're thrown against the shield. A trickle of blood snakes down his sweaty forehead when we land. I open my mouth to ask if he's all right, to demand an explanation for his protecting me, but the words change before I can utter them. "Watch out, Viper!" I point at a crack starting at the circle's edge and spreading along the ground through its center. Cleaving it in two.

Ignoring my last attempt to stop it, the dark brown cord of River's earth magic pulls free of the now unraveling weave and descends upon the shifting earth. The ground cracks beneath the pressure, and what started as a small crack erupts into a five-pace-wide fissure that swallows Viper into its darkness.

7

TYE

The ground rumbled beneath Tye, the earthquake violent enough to knock him on his back. By the time he rolled to his feet, his mouth gritty with hot sand, the world had changed.

Where the sands of the arena had stretched across flat land, now a grand fissure cracked the field in two. The lips of the new canyon rose higher than Tye's head, the lacerated earth showing its rocky entrails. And in the middle of it all, bisected by the new abyss, stood a shimmering wall that encircled his Lilac Girl and Viper.

"Leralynn," Tye shouted, filling the arena with his bellow.

No answer. Not even a distant whimper.

Coal was already there, staring up at the wall, punching it hard enough to break bone. Tye sprinted toward him as fast as he could in the loose sand. When he arrived, Coal turned blazing blue eyes on him and shook his head. Impenetrable.

With a growl, Tye launched himself at the closest of Viper's blue-clad quint mates, grasping the male's tunic to lift him into the air. "What the hell is that?" Tye demanded, throwing the male into the silver wall so hard that he heard the sound of skull striking metal.

"Static shield," the male answered quickly from the ground, holding up his palms. His eyes were wide, his face pale against his pitch-black hair, the smell of fear flowing from him in waves. "We used a ward to tie up all our magics into a shield. We just wanted to separate you. The earthquake isn't our doing."

Lera.

Ice gripped Tye's chest. The lass had held four cords of magic, panicked, and lost her grip on them. And the one thing he could have done to help increase her control—coupling— he'd selfishly refused.

All because he had fallen in love, soul and all, and wanted as much in return. Tye wanted to *mate*, and in longing for that unattainable bond, he'd put the lass in danger.

A dull roaring filled his ears as he stared at the shimmering wall. Lera was in there. Alone. Perhaps hurt. Certainly scared. Raising his hand, Tye encircled the male's neck with a collar of flames, holding it so close to the bastard's skin that it would burn him at the slightest of motions. "Take your shield down. *Now.*"

"Tye," River called from across the split in the earth, his voice cutting through Tye's haze, too calm and steady for reality. River held a panting warrior by one arm. "Let him go. The shield is static—they can't take it down. It will hold for . . . How long is the ward for?" River snapped the last words at the male in his grip.

"An hour." The male swallowed. "Our quint had no chance to beat you. We knew it, you knew it. Viper just wanted to show the council that we tried. Lure the girl away, separate you. Make you twiddle your thumbs for an hour. No one was to get hurt."

Tye let the collar tighten, scorching the male's skin. The smell of burnt flesh rose into the air, together with a bit-back scream. "Now someone *is* hurt." Tye's harsh voice sounded foreign even to his own ears. "So call a surrender and end this now."

"Can't." The male held still despite the pain, sweat running down his temples and into his eyes. "We don't have a surrender left. If we try, the runes will kill us."

"Let him go." Coal grabbed Tye's wrist, though Tye little remembered the warrior moving toward him.

"Why?"

Coal shifted his weight, placing himself directly before Tye, his blue eyes clear and fierce. In another world, the notion of Coal talking Tye down from violence would have been hilarious. Now, it was just noise.

"Because Viper's quint played by the rules," Coal said quietly. "There was no malice. Until now. Until you."

Rules. A phantom hand squeezed Tye's soul, digging daggers into his heart. Yes, he'd played by the bloody rules once. Right up until they turned on him. Snapped him in two. Lera, so full of life and goodness—she deserved better than the broken male Tye was. He should have slept with her and been grateful, and then he should have let her go.

Coal's grip tightened, bending Tye's wrist so painfully that he dropped to his knees beneath the pressure, making the black-haired male moan in fresh pain. With no change in his stony expression, Coal stared down at him, silently pulling rank. "Stand down, you imbecile, and channel what passes for brains into finding a way over this wall. It is infinitely more efficient if you leave murder to me. I'm better at it." The last came under Coal's breath, likely not intended to be said aloud at all.

Tye's nostrils flared but he released Viper's quint mate, who scrambled away with a sharp gasp.

Coal nodded and eased the pressure on Tye's joint, though he didn't let go completely, as if afraid Tye might attack someone else. Coal was smart that way. "The wall is too smooth to climb," he said, jerking his chin at the shimmering shield rising fifteen feet into the air behind him. "Could your tiger clear it?"

Tye's stomach turned. Yes, the tiger could clear the wall— maybe. At least enough to get his paws hooked over the top rim. But Tye couldn't make the animal choose to do so. Just as Tye could do nothing to stop the tiger from attacking everyone in the arena. Tye had failed the tiger just as he'd failed Lera, trading the needs of the developing bond as a colt for something he'd wanted—the heady thrill of flex—only to end up with nothing at all.

"Tye." Coal's eyes flashed with blue ice. "I asked—"

Rolling his wrist to free it of Coal's hold, Tye spread his chest and snarled at the other male. "I heard you. And no, the tiger can't make the bloody jump."

8

LERA

"Viper!" Not trusting my legs, I crawl up the raised lip of the crack. Sand grinds into my cuts and I grit my teeth against the pain. An endlessly deep wedge stares back at me, its walls made of crumbling orange and red stone that disappears eventually into blackness. Heat wafts from the crack like the earth's core itself has been exposed. "Viper!"

My voice echoes and ricochets down the walls like a tossed pebble.

"Here." The male's tight voice draws my eyes to a tiny ledge fifteen feet down from where I kneel. Standing on one leg, Viper grips a nub of a handhold. His other leg, bent at an unnatural angle, hangs off the side of the abyss. He curses and releases one hand to work the flag loose from his belt. Still worrying about winning the damn trial.

"Neither of us has a surrender left," Viper says, as if having heard my thought. His voice strains, the words coming in gasps. "Don't want the flag to fall with me. No need for your quint to die."

I swallow, my hands digging into the rock. "You aren't falling anywhere until I say you are," I call down, sounding more like Coal or River than myself. My stomach clenches at the need to have the males close, but I shove the ache away. I have to. For Viper's sake.

A pained chuckle reaches me. "A mortal is giving me orders?"

I run my hand along the red stone. Soft. Porous. Unstable. And the only option to save Viper's life. "A *weaver* is giving you orders." My heart beats so hard, it's a wonder the rock doesn't tremble from it. "And after this trial is over, I'll outrank you, won't I?"

Silence answers me.

"Viper!" I survey the deadly drop in search of a way down.

"Yes." The word comes soft and blurry, the male's strength draining with each heartbeat.

"Yes, *what?*" *There.* A two-foot-wide ledge, just above Viper's tenuous hold. If I can get to it, I could lower something for Viper to hold on to. Anchor him in. Except there's a dozen feet of crumbling stone between the ledge and me, with death waiting for me to slip. "Viper. Yes, *what?*"

"Yes, ma'am," the male says, not even fighting the insult. Damn it.

I look at my trembling hands, the knuckles still bleeding from trying to punch the shield. My breath comes in quick puffs, my pulse sprinting, my mouth dry and filled with specks of earth. Before my courage fails completely, I swing myself over the edge, sending sand and small stones into the abyss before me.

"What the bloody hell are you doing?" Viper's suddenly awake voice cracks the air. "One death isn't enough? You need to make it two?"

"Your confidence in me is overwhelm—" The lip I'm holding crumbles, my body sliding two feet along sharp, brittle stone before I find footing, my hands gripping tiny nubs of rock. *Stars.* Am I imagining it or is it already hotter here? I can't breathe for the tightness in my chest, the sinking feeling in my gut.

"Leralynn!" Viper calls.

"I'm all right." I'm not all right. I'm going to die. But he doesn't need to know that. I lay my cheek against the rock, forcing air into my spasming lungs. Once. Twice. On the third inhale, I close my eyes to wash away the abyss and focus on nothing but the rock beneath me. Think. Feel. Stay alive. Keep Viper alive.

Gently reaching down with my leg, I find the next foothold and tap the outcropping with my boot before entrusting my weight to it. I feel for the next. The next. My arms ache, my already bleeding fingers leaving wet proof of my descent. Ten feet to go until the ledge. Eight. Six. I press my hips against the rock wall, trying to take pressure off my screaming arms.

My grip fails just as I reach for a solid hold, my fingers refusing to hold on for a moment longer. With a scream, I fall the rest of the way to the ledge. The thud of impact comes first, a numbness and dull ringing that echo through my body. Then pain. A hot knife driving into my ankle, lines of fire along my shin. The world wavers. Blackens.

My first, ridiculous thought is how mad Coal will be about my foiled landing. My next is a list of increasingly crude variations on the "I told you I wasn't ready" I will scream at the bastard.

"Leralynn?" The weakness in Viper's voice parts the veil of darkness clouding my vision.

Get Viper first. Die second. Yell at Coal in between.

Dirt coating my tongue, I breathe in the chalky dust with every gasp. But I do breathe. Do push myself up onto my hands and knees, even as my skin burns, sweat and blood wetting my clothes. Making myself look down, I find the top of Viper's hand two feet below me—and a chasm of black nothing beyond.

With jerky motions, I unfasten my belt. Looping one end around my wrist, I extend the rest down to the injured male. "Grab on."

Instead of reaching for the leather, Viper strains his head back, turquoise eyes wild with pain. "Do you have purchase?" he gasps. "Don't want to pull you down."

"There's a spike here. I'm anchored in with my armor." I grit my teeth, making myself believe my own lie before Viper sees through it. "Stop stalling and use the damn belt to climb up before I decide you aren't worth the trouble."

Viper's hand moves off the stone, the nub of rock he'd been holding breaking off with the shift of weight. For a second, he hangs over the abyss, one foot and one hand his only anchors to life. Then he grips the belt, and my shoulder roars as I brace his climb.

The sight of my enemy quint leader pulling himself up beside me on the ledge is one of the most beautiful things I've ever seen. Tipping my head up to the arena's sky, I make a crude gesture that I hope Klarissa knows is meant for her. Beside me, Viper chuckles softly and rests his back against the stone.

"So what now?" I ask.

"Now we wait. The static shield will go down in thirty minutes or so and our quints will charge in with a grand rescue. Then you get to win, and we go to breakfast."

Silence falls.

Viper's breath is coming in short gasps now, his skin gray and clammy.

"Bet you wish you'd made it one of those half-hour shields, huh?" I say.

Viper looks at me with wide eyes and suddenly we're both laughing.

"Just so you know, mortal," he says once the absurd mirth dies away to silence and the throbbing of our wounds rises to fill the void. "You won more than my flag today. The magic made no mistake when it chose you for Lunos."

9

LERA

"You used the life-and-death-defining flag as a handkerchief?" Shaking his head, River sets me on the edge of the worktable in the preparation room, the arena's cheering still echoing in my ears.

"I needed to wipe my face." I try to smile and grimace instead. "Viper and I had little other use for it at the time." My body hurts. My head aches. A hot knife stabs my ankle every time I dare shift my weight. I can feel the other males close by, resisting the urge to crowd me, per River's orders—Tye pacing restlessly, Coal making himself busy over armor, Shade laying out medical supplies with thunder in his golden eyes. I count them all, over and over, needing the reassurance that they are all right.

"Indeed." River brushes hair from my face, his sweat-soaked temples and mussed, sandy hair probably a mirror of my own.

"I could have killed you. I nearly did kill Viper." I shoot Coal a dark look. "You still think the council was right?"

A muscle in Coal's jaw ticks once, then he tosses his armor polish into a wooden crate and walks out the door, the slam echoing in his wake.

"Coal!" I groan, starting after him only to have River's heavy hand hold me in place. "It was a bloody jest."

"Today's trial . . . It was the longest hour of my life, Leralynn," River says quietly. "Standing on the other side of that shield, unable to get to you. I don't remember ever being so terrified as that. And I doubt Coal can either. Give him time to work through it."

I lean my head against River, breathing in his earthy scent. My cheek brushes the smooth skin of his neck, now clear of runes. It's over. It's actually over. The trials, the Citadel, Klarissa's unchecked power over us. I try to understand it, to let it sink through me that we're finally an official, sanctioned quint. That we can finally leave this polished, poisonous Citadel. Leave and never return.

Except, of course, it *isn't* over. I'm too slow to hide my shudder.

"What is it?" River's gaze pierces mine.

"I want to feel like something monumental just finished, but the truth is that it's all just starting, isn't it? What we have to do before Lunos is safe."

River nods, his thumb tracing my cheek. "True. For now, however, let's get you back on your feet." He looks over his shoulder at where Shade has finished organizing salves, bandages, and several unpleasant-looking implements on a tray. "Why don't we take her to the baths?"

Shade shakes his head. "Not until I have the ankle stabilized." Leaving off his preparations, he comes up beside River and lays a hand against the side of my face. His yellow eyes are clear and focused, his emotions held back at a low simmer just as his black hair is caught in a tail. Shade's healer mode. "I'm sorry, cub. We've a bit of mending to do before you can go anywhere." He leans forward to kiss my forehead before returning to his work. I close my eyes momentarily at the warmth left behind by his velvet-soft lips and the lingering scent of damp forest, wishing he'd stayed there longer.

Taking up the space Shade vacated, Tye crouches beside me, his lithe muscles rippling beneath a torn tunic. Once the static shield fell, the male had scampered down the rock with such feline grace and so little concern for gravity that even Viper loosed an appreciative whistle. Now, all that power seems contained behind piercing green eyes. It's intoxicating, after all his distance and avoidance these past few days, to have his full attention on me. I wonder what it means—probably just the emotion of the trial burning through him. Reaching up, he takes my hands in his, the pads of his thumbs running lightly over my damaged knuckles. "I want to sleep with you."

"What?" I jerk back and instantly regret the motion as pain from my head, ankle, and cut-up skin collide. "Now?"

"No. Yes." Tye cringes. "If I'd not been a selfish idiot about it, all of this might have been different. Stars. Lilac Girl . . . I'm . . ."

"If you think yourself responsible for the earthquake I started, you give your cock entirely too much credit," I mutter.

Tye's face lowers, the pain in his sharp features squeezing my heart. I wish I understood what was going on in that mind of his. "I don't know what to say, lass."

"That is usually a good sign to shut up," Shade says from where he strips away my bootlaces. "And if we are to have a chance of riding out of here today, I suggest you leave me to my work. Unless your cock has suddenly developed healing powers?"

Tye rocks back on his heels. "No, that would be *Coal's*. I'm keeping track, you know."

The tips of my ears heat, turning into spasming chuckles when the male wiggles his brows. I try to hold back the laughter for the sake of my abused bones, but the first *ha* escapes with the force of a rearing stallion. My back arches and I grab Tye's hand, squeezing it in an attempt to steady my body.

It's no use, not when the tension of the past hours breaks whatever dam held it back and spills out in a storm. "'Keeping . . . track,'" I gasp. "You . . . are . . . insufferable." My laughter fills the preparation room, deep and desperate and unstoppable, even when tears finally start streaming down my dusty cheeks.

TRUE TO HIS WORD, River keeps us at the Citadel not a moment longer than he must. Trading a celebratory dinner for a few extra hours of daylight, we pack our things and head for the stable just as the bell tolls four in the afternoon. I savor my last walk across the Citadel grounds, inhaling the sweet, wine-scented air, the bustle of warriors-in-training. I won't miss it, but I can appreciate its unfettered beauty now that I'm leaving.

The smell of horses and hay carried on a lively breeze greets me like an old friend. The ivy growing around the long wooden rafters floats on a breeze from the open door, and far overhead, the magically lit lanterns still give their steady glow, even in broad daylight. I long to wrap my arms around Sprite, but she's occupied at the moment—the gray mare eyes Coal's unamused stallion as the warrior checks both sets of tack.

Standing with his arms behind his back, River listens to

something Klarissa is saying. The female's gown, the color of honey, hugs her slender hips and tangles seductively around her ankles. Stars, even the female's dress seems intent on inviting River into her bed. When Klarissa extends a hand toward River's cheek, a bitterness fills my mouth.

River steps back, out of reach.

Klarissa's smile tightens.

She looks in my direction, gives me a tiny quirk of her perfect red lips and a delicate farewell wave, then breezes out the door without waiting for my response.

I run my fingers over my rune-free neck and my own new outfit, which Autumn put together with a child's delight. The embroidered forest-green tunic is both tight and flexible, the low, scooped neckline managing to look sensual instead of lewd. A silver pendant of a dragon—a gift from Shade to celebrate the trial conclusion—hangs just above the swell of my breasts, while Coal's finest knife sits in a clever sheath attached to my thigh for ease of access.

Autumn hands me a fur-lined cloak, a gentle smile on her face. She's resplendent in a close-fitting white travel outfit and a long white cape. "I know it doesn't seem like it now, but the mountain path will get downright freezing. Are you certain you want to stay with the males instead of traveling with Kora and me? The bastards want to trek through the Light for two weeks, all in the name of—what was it, River?"

"Prudence," River calls over. "I want to be at full strength at the palace and get eyes on the land meanwhile—and let the land get eyes on me. I'm hoping that if Griorgi's spies spot us on our way to Slait, he might even beat us there instead of us having to draw him out."

"Yes, well, it sounds like you have plenty of eyes to go around, so you don't need mine." Autumn tosses her braids over her shoulder and gives me a sympathetic look. "I know the Gloom seeps energy, but so do the cold and wind. I want to have life's basic necessities."

"Basic necessities like a library?" I ask.

"Precisely." Motioning for me to spin around, the female takes charge of my unruly auburn locks.

"Did you have too many dolls growing up?" I ask, feeling confident hands tug along my scalp.

"There is no such thing as too many dolls." Autumn lowers her voice. "Can you believe Kora will let me choose none of her clothes? I brought out some lip paint yesterday and she ran away faster than Tye at the sight of a book. You are my last hope."

"I take it you've relented to Kora tagging along while we dethrone the king of Slait, reseal Jawrar inside Mors, and turn our relationship with the Elders Council on its head?"

"Only because I promised to bring chocolate on the ride," Kora says, stepping up beside Autumn and me. The tall warrior's blue eyes survey the departure preparations, softening as they fall on Autumn. "Though I'm not sure where it will fit, considering the number of books she'd like to bring along. Could we discuss whether borrowing half of the Citadel's holdings and transporting them to Slait is . . . prudent for such fragile and valuable texts?"

Swallowing a snort, I excuse myself from the pair only to spot Shade entering the stable yard.

My body tenses at once, the thin beat of my heart echoing through my muscles, which suddenly can't decide between freezing or bolting. The two hours Shade spent working on me earlier, mercilessly clearing debris from gashes, setting bones, and driving sharp needles through injured flesh (to lay the groundwork for the subsequent—and little more pleasant—

magical healing) make me unable to look at rocks without blanching. Much less at the male himself.

Suddenly I'm aware of a dull throbbing in my ankle, a cut on my shoulder where one of the stitches came open, the intermittent zings of pain that will make sitting tall in the saddle difficult—each injury a healer's target as surely as a bullseye is an archer's. Unable to stop myself, I step back. Instead of escaping, I hit a hard body, its slightly metallic male scent mixed with a horse's sweetness. Coal. Who was with the horses until moments ago. Heat rises to my face, tingling in my ears. Caught in the act: a warrior who fears healers. Having Shade understand the truth of it is bad enough; to have Coal realize what's happening stretches the limits of humiliation.

"Cub." Shade's yellow eyes soften in sympathy as he approaches. Wearing soft black pants and a gray cashmere sweater that clings to his hard chest, black hair loose at his shoulders, he is the perfect mix of wolf and fae. Soft warmth sheathing deadly teeth. Stunning golden eyes that pull you in —and can follow you in the dark. Velvety, tan skin covering muscles that could break your neck with a single jerk. What was it that Coal said once? *Don't let Shade's good table manners distract you from what he eats for dinner.* "Let me take another look at you before we go."

"Of course. In a moment. Excuse me." I try to wriggle out of Coal's hands, which have settled heavily on my shoulders. "I need to relieve myself."

"No, you don't." Coal's low, gravelly voice brushes the back of my neck, the heat of his body a shield against the wind. "You are as bad a liar as Tye claims."

Lovely. Where is River's earth-opening magic when I need it?

Turning me toward him, Coal puts a callused finger under

my chin, lifting my flaming face to meet his cool blue eyes—looking at me for the first time since storming out of the preparation room hours ago, though his chiseled face reveals nothing of his thoughts.

I tense.

Coal's eyes skitter over my shoulder for a moment, no doubt to examine Shade's, before returning.

My heart stutters, a new heat filling me despite everything going on around us. I bite my lip, a small defense against the force of Coal's mere presence. I've met no other being who wields silence the way the warrior before me does, and that alone quickens my breath.

"Pain that you cannot defend yourself against is the worst kind," he says quietly, dropping those shields of his to let me see the understanding in his eyes. Images tap my mind softly. Shackles. A whip. And then another: Shade's hand glowing with silver magic while the rest of the quint pins me—no, pins *Coal*—against the ground. "When I had just come through the wall, I hated Shade very much."

I bite my lip. "Not just me, then?"

"Not at all." Coal's muscles tighten. "I tried to shove my way into more risk than you might have otherwise taken this morning. And I see you are paying for the consequences still. That, at least, I might be able to do something about."

Bending his head, Coal presses his mouth over mine. His masculine scent and taste surround me. The intensity of his lips rouses each of my exhausted nerves to alert, my hands rising to dig into the hard swells of his biceps. A heartbeat later, a phantom power stirs inside me, mirroring the sudden swelling of my breasts and a gripping need low in my belly. The throbbing in my ankle quiets. An energy that's an echo of

Coal's magic seeps new strength into tired muscles, masking the pain and ache.

"Coal." Shade's rough reprimand has Coal's hand tangling in my hair as he pauses to lift a brow at the shifter. Behind me, Shade growls softly.

I do too.

"There is a cost to her echoing your magic." The usually gentle male sounds like the wolf he is. A predator defending his territory—not me, but my wellbeing. "Lera's body will echo your strength and healing for a bit, and then she will crash even lower than now. Any more mending needs to be done the old-fashioned way until her body recovers. Let me have her."

"Poke and prod her again just now and the mortal will slug you," Coal says evenly. "And I will help her. Go. Away."

A growl and flash of light are Shade's only answer. As Coal's mouth descends upon mine, however, I catch sight of a gray wolf lifting his leg to urinate over Coal's scabbard, his black muzzle pulled back over long white teeth. Wrapping my hands in Coal's hair before he can notice as much, I meet his demanding kiss with a force of my own. Our tongues clash inside our joined mouths, the battle making my hips press against Coal's hardness, my body singing with new strength.

The last coherent thought I have before releasing the waking beast inside me is the realization that I haven't seen Tye in hours. I shove away the worry for him, the pain, the questions, and just let myself live in the now for a bit longer.

10

TYE

*L*eaning against the wooden fence, Tye let the breeze brush the hair from his face. Far away from the brewing departure preparations, the sand-filled sparring ring was silent but for the slight whistle of the wind. That and the ghosts.

He hadn't been able to get to her. To go through the static shield, for its impenetrable magic. Or jump over it, for his own deficiency. Worse, the whole mishap had been his fault. Tye knew the strength of his magic, the wildness in it that rivaled any stallion. No, stallion was too domesticated a term. Tye's magic had the visceral needs of the tiger without any of the safeguards of the fae male. That's what he'd given Lera to wrestle with while holding back the one act that might have helped her control the force.

Lera got hurt. And it wasn't the first time someone Tye cared for had been injured over his choices.

Digging his fingers into the fence, Tye stared at the horizontal bar that someone had lugged from the practice arena to this unused spot. Even standing at the fence, Tye could feel the smooth flex of the bar, smell the chalk that always made a mess no matter how careful one was, taste the exhilaration of flying through the air, his magic and his muscles singing. It was all there for the taking.

A piece of cheese in a mousetrap.

The sound of familiar rolling footsteps behind Tye was simultaneously unexpected and inevitable. Tye still didn't understand how Elidyr had managed to train in flex when he seemed unable to walk quite right without a horse beneath him. Hell, Tye wouldn't even believe it possible if he'd not seen Elidyr compete for himself.

Elidyr had competed on the flex-air circuit, as Tye had on the flex-fire track. At his peak, the elder had been a few tiers below Tye, but that in itself was an achievement few could claim. As for the level Tye had been at, well, things had looked very different from up there.

Leaning against the fence beside Tye, Elidyr let the stallion he was holding graze on the lush grass. "Miss it?" he asked, holding a long strand of hay between his teeth.

There was little point in feigning misunderstanding, so Tye didn't bother. "No."

"I could have sworn I saw you enjoying yourself there for a moment, before class started," Elidyr drawled, a smile cracking his tan, oval face. "Flying through your routine, defying death, stretching the full control and precision of your power."

"Aye." Tye turned around and leaned back on his arms. Anyone else, he'd have told to pound sand—elder or not. But Elidyr had lived and breathed the sport for a solid century, and the pull of professional courtesy made Tye indulge the male's questions longer than he would have otherwise. "But I presumed you were asking whether I miss the lifestyle, not a few flips when no one is watching."

"And you don't?"

"Do I miss spending ten hours a day in practice, most of it in one agony or another? Listening to the healer warn me time and time again that if I sustain one more injury to my shoulder or my magic or my spine, there won't be enough power in Lunos to piece me back together? Being called three kinds of imbecile over and over?"

"Heh." Elidyr clicked his tongue. "From where the rest of us stood, you were one breath away from a god. There wasn't one athlete there who didn't worship the ground you walked on. Who wouldn't have traded anything to be you."

"Yes, well, it always looks more glamorous from the side." Especially since, at the end, none of Tye's skill or training had mattered. "Pity party over. What can I do for you, sir?"

Elidyr's bay stallion nuzzled the male's hip, rubbing against it with enough force to have knocked a lesser being off his feet. The elder spread his shoulders, glaring at the horse until the latter stepped back and lowered his head. "Better." Elidyr scratched the animal's head before returning his attention to Tye. "It occurred to me that I owe you an apology. That perhaps when I helped twist your arm into teaching flex to the trainees, I didn't fully comprehend the wounds it would open."

"I was a Citadel initiate. Your order was fully lawful." Tye raised his face to the wind. "There's nothing to apologize for."

Elidyr clicked his tongue. "Something happened right before the championship you never came to."

"The whole of Lunos knows what happened, Eli. I got drunk enough to be thrown in a cell and I missed my start time."

"Hmm." Elidyr made a noncommittal noise, his attention

73

back on the horse, idly stroking his neck with a callused hand. "I did hear that. Occurred to me after watching you teach class that mayhap there was more to it. That perhaps your quint brothers know as little of the truth as I do."

Tye stuck his hands into the pockets of his leather riding pants and grinned. Coal might think brooding silence was the most efficient way to get intrusive bastards off one's back, but in truth, cockiness worked a great deal better. "I assure you that my quint brothers know more about my past than my own mother." He cut a conspiratorial glance toward the other male. "Point of fact, I think the notion of making us do two extra trials to make up for my indiscretions was your idea. I hope I never accidentally thanked you for it."

The expected bark of laughter didn't come. Not good. Inside his pockets, Tye's hands clenched into fists.

"You should tell them," Elidyr said, flipping the horse's reins into place and swinging lightly into the saddle. "At least that female of yours."

Tye's jaw clenched, his anger surging to the surface one moment before he would have been in the clear. "You and Klarissa did a fine job of running my personal business up the bloody flagpole for all to see. You'll forgive me if I little want your advice on what else I should be doing."

"Tye—" Elidyr started, but Tye stepped into the Gloom and drowned out the elder.

11

LERA

I only realize how tight my chest has been when I take my first breath of pine-filled freedom. Sprite's saddle shifts beneath me as the silent hinges of the Citadel's intricate metal gate close at our backs, the blindingly white wall rising above us. Despite being barely audible, the click of the lock reverberates through me like thunder. Through everyone.

I bite my lip, watching my males gather together a few paces down the uneven slope. The packed-dirt road winds down before us, lined with brilliant maples and ash trees, hidden birds chattering all around. It feels like only yesterday that the five of us wound our way up here, certain we'd be leaving in a matter of days to do as we pleased—not riding out weeks later to dethrone one of the most powerful males in Lunos.

Shade, traveling in wolf form, keeps his distance from the horses, but they stomp the ground nonetheless, huffing their anxiety to get moving. The males' stallions are majestic in the late-afternoon sun, their heads held high, their powerful muscles vibrating with pride and energy. Just like the males sitting atop them. The males who went to the Citadel for me. Who lowered to their knees and bent their heads to accept runes and trials and humiliations that should have been centuries behind them.

Only now that we are leaving the Citadel do I truly feel the magnitude of their sacrifice.

"Is something amiss, lass?" Tye calls to me over the wind. The cool breeze clears his red hair from his eyes, green and mischievous and tinged with a sadness I can't crack. The male appeared at the stable only moments ago, giving us all his cocky grin and a simple, "Well, what are waiting for?" I thought the thunder in River's eyes might bring the building down around us; he'd been readying to search the Citadel himself.

I nod, surveying the rippling treetops and jagged mountains that surround us. And far below in the valley, the green meadows and dense forests spreading across the neutral lands toward Slait. Nature in its raw magnificence. Nudging Sprite up beside the red-haired male, I take his hand and bring it to my face, rubbing my cheek against his rough knuckles. "Tye—"

"Pick up your reins, mortal, or I swear I'll take you on a bloody lead line," Coal says, his voice wedging between Tye and me.

I give Coal a vulgar gesture but do take up the leather. With that, River picks up the pace and leads us toward home.

JUST A FEW MILES outside the Citadel, River's other reason for insisting we travel alone through the mountains becomes clear. As we enter the thick forest that blankets the mountain range, Tye reins in beside Coal and swings out of the saddle, handing off his horse to the black-clad warrior.

"Where—"

River shakes his head at me, a worried look on his face.

My chest tightens, squeezing more painfully still when, without so much as looking toward me, Tye disappears into the pines. A few moments later, a bright light flashes between the branches and the rustling of a great tiger loping through the trees reaches our small clearing. The spots of orange amidst the green flash by like stars in a night sky. I stare at the bright spots as they get farther away, realizing I've gone rigid only when the horse beneath me dances her discontent.

"Sorry, girl." Eyes still on the forest, I swing out of the saddle to land on the hard-packed earth, my muscles whining in protest. After not riding at the Citadel, even the past hour in the saddle has taken its toll.

"Do you intend to walk to Slait?" Coal asks.

"Do you intend to be an ass all the way to Slait, or are you balancing some cosmic normal-being versus horrid-jerk scale that your kiss upset?" I shoot back at him, watching his sharply carved jaw clench at the kiss's mention. At the dagger-sharp condemnation in the wolf's yellow gaze, clear even from ten yards away.

Brilliant. Less than a day from the Citadel, and one male is prancing off into the woods without so much as an explanation while another is reverting back to walling himself off, probably in deference to some idiotic "protect Lera from myself" logic. I rub my eyes with the heels of my hands and focus on the gurgle of a nearby river. "Forget it. I'll go fill the water skins while we wait. Do you want to give me yours?"

Coal snorts. "One, that's salt water you're hearing, running from a spring in the White Cliffs. Two"—he holds up his fingers as if concerned I'll be too daft to follow—"Tye won't be back for at least a week. And three, either get back in the saddle or walk, but we aren't halting here much longer."

"A *week*?" My mouth dries when River nods in agreement.

"There are few places safe for Tye's tiger to roam loose," he says, his attention on the forest. "And he's gone too long without doing so. I think it might be one of the reasons he's been so . . . not himself lately. Since we're out here, we might as well use the time." He clicks his horse forward, looking back when I don't follow right away. "Come, Leralynn. The beast will likely stay in our vicinity as we move—roughly—but I want to put as much distance between us and the Citadel as possible before we bed down for the night, in case he strays."

Now that we're not within the high walls of the Citadel, I can see River pulling his commander's cloak even closer around him. We're loose in the dangerous neutral lands, and the weight of our survival here rests on his too-tight shoulders.

By the time River finally calls a halt, Shade's prediction about the effects of Coal's magic on my body comes true with a vengeance. I grip the saddle to keep from toppling over as Sprite walks, and I don't fall on my face dismounting only because Shade lifts me off the horse—ensuring that Coal sees him do it. The blond warrior's jaw tightens, and I can practically see the wall rising higher around him. The useless, punishing thoughts that I can't make him un-think. *Lera is hurt. My fault. My fault. My fault.*

"Stop it." I shove Shade's chest. Lose what little balance my wobbling legs were granting me. Fall right in front of Coal's boots, nearly re-twisting my ankle in the process.

I catch a flash of alarm in Coal's eyes, which he shutters

just as quickly. He bends to help me up, but Shade blocks him with an arm.

"Next time I tell you what you may or may not do with my patient, you listen," Shade says, his quiet murmur as full of command as River's. He waits a beat, letting the order sink in. "Gather firewood. We'll need some tonight."

I open my mouth to protest, but Coal is gone before I can conjure words. My body surrenders to tremors despite everything I can do to keep them at bay. River wraps a cloak around me, guiding me into a mountain cave that looks like little more than a massive black blob to my mortal eyes. I run my hands along the damp wall, inhaling the scents of earth and moss. By the time Coal returns with wood and makes short work of a fire, I'm tucked securely against the cave wall, keeping my mouth shut as Shade examines my ankle and several of the deeper gashes, taking each aggravated cut as a personal affront.

"You can't do anything for her?" River asks Shade, settling with his arm around me.

"If you mean with magic, nothing that won't make things worse in the long term." Shade brushes a lock of hair from my face, his yellow eyes softening. "You can push a body to heal faster like you can nudge a horse into a quicker gallop—only to a point. It's all right for you to need a bit of rest, cub. No one expects you to pretend the trial never happened, that you aren't sore. Okay? Can you let us just hold you for a night?"

"Don't bother answering," River says, pulling me closer against his side, his heat and strength cocooning me. "I'm holding you whether you let me or not."

I'm still sitting upright when I drift off to sleep.

～

I wake to River's heavy arm around me, thin dawn light pressing against my eyelids, and the smell of blood filling my nose. I'm so used to the coppery scent from my own wounds by now that for a moment I simply snuggle deeper into River's warm, bare chest, his smooth muscles shifting tighter around me. Then the blood hits me again, stronger.

Opening my eyes, I stare at a pair of glazed dead ones and scream, my mind still processing the scene. Coal is on his feet immediately, sword drawn, blond hair loose against bunched shoulders. Heart pounding, I sit up to behold the freshly killed rabbit that one of the juvenile bastards decided to drop off inches away from my face. "Shade!"

"It wasn't me." Shade blinks his long lashes at me from his spot by the mouth of the cave. "I'd have brought a pair at least. How poor a hunter do you think I am?"

Shoving the dead rabbit into the shifter's chest, I pull on my boots and walk down to a nearby creek, which at least flows with fresh—if freezing—water. Between Tye running off, Shade's told-you-so healer persona, and Coal pulling back more each hour, my sense of humor is taking a bloody beating. Maybe there's a plant somewhere that makes wolves itch. Yes, that would have been a better way of going about the morning.

Savoring that prospect, I scoop water with cupped hands and splash my face quickly. The icy cold grips my lungs at once, and it takes several breaths before I can look at the creek again. In the clear water, my own reflection stares back at me.

That, and the furry face of a green-eyed tiger.

1 2

LERA

*B*reath held, I turn slowly. Very, very slowly.

Taking a step forward, the tiger drops a dead hare at my feet and proceeds to the water, lowering his head to lap his fill from the creek.

I swallow. "Tye? Can you understand me?"

No answer, bar the rhythmic swoosh of his black-tipped tail.

"I'll take that as a no," I mutter, retreating one step, then another.

The tiger's head lifts and swings toward me, sunlight sculpting the lithe muscles beneath his velvety fur. His green eyes narrow on me, slide for an instant to the hare I left untouched, then return lazily to the water, where he resumes his lapping.

I don't see Tye again as I help pack up the campsite and go through a training bout with Coal, who currently seems willing to converse with me only through practice swords—which today strike neither quickly nor hard. By the time we're in the saddle, Czar seems to have absorbed enough of his rider's mood to snap his teeth at anyone riding beside him—poor Sprite included. Keeping the mare back, I survey the path for any sign of feline company. There is none.

Until that evening, that is, when I return to camp from taking care of my needs to find a dead deer atop my saddlebags.

Bile crawls up my throat at the sight of viscous deer blood soaking through my bags and into the clothes inside. "Oh, stars." Clamping my hands over my mouth, I try to keep from breathing in the thick, coppery scent. "That is disgusting."

Shade heaves the carcass away from my things, bare arms hardly even straining. "That is dinner delivery."

Picking up a small stone from the ground, I launch it with all my strength at Shade's shoulder. The male takes the hit with a grunt and a smirk. "Will you not be skinning it yourself, then?"

Refusing to dignify the bastard with a response, I pull the blood-soaked clothes from my bags and, not wanting to pollute the small drinking stream, start for the river well downhill from the campsite. With the clear sky, River opted to spend the night in the thick forest instead of the oppressive mountainside caves, which—until just now—was going to mean less trekking up and down the slope.

"You've about an hour of light left," Shade calls after me. "Be careful."

"I did somehow manage to keep track of the sun before meeting you, Shade," I call over my shoulder to the overprotective male. At least Tye chose the evening time to leave his offering, which means the laundry has a fighting chance of drying overnight. That, or turning into sheets of ice.

Navigating prickly pine branches and horse-sized boulders, I finally come to the water, which rushes quickly over smooth stones. With the vast horizon on one side and a great snowcapped mountain rising on the other, the beauty of Lunos settles like a shawl over my shoulders. Finding a rock that's both large enough to spread out my things and far enough into the river that I can reach the swiftly flowing water without actually having to step into it, I dump my laundry beside me. Three shirts and two sets of pants, all soaked through with deer blood and—

My foot slips on a wet patch of rock and I throw out my arms, barely keeping myself from tumbling into the water— but still landing atop the soiled laundry. "Damn it." My breath comes in pants as I examine my stinging left forearm, where a long bloody gash runs from wrist to elbow. Adding insult to injury, deer blood now soaks into my breeches. Holding the wound against my mouth, I sit back on my heels and growl at the cold sky.

An animal growls back.

"Not now, Tye," I say without turning around. "You are at least partially responsible for all this, you know."

Behind me, the growl comes again, this time with the *click, click, click* of claws against stone. Then . . . nothing.

A cold shiver runs along the length of my spine, the rushing of the river suddenly too quiet. "Tye?" Slipping my knife from its sheath on my thigh, I stand and slowly turn around.

The tiger is there, two paces away.

"Stars, cat, I thought it was someone else," I say, letting the familiar green eyes and swishing tail soothe my nerves as I re-sheathe the blade.

The tiger's nostrils flare, his eyes narrowing on the drops of blood coming from my arm. At the deer blood saturating my scent. The tail stops swishing. His ears perk and still.

I swallow, a fine tremor of fear rushing through me, my muscles waking with the need to be elsewhere. Now.

The tiger advances, his great maw of white teeth glistening in the evening light. A large pink tongue jets out to lick a twitching nose. The click of claws on stone reverberates through my body as the predator's focus zeros in on my blood again. When the tiger lets free a roar, there is a different sound to it. One that I've not heard before.

Marking my escape route, I slide slowly to the side.

The tiger shifts his weight to block my path, sharp green eyes missing nothing.

Behind me, the icy, rushing river beats against the rocks. In front of me, there is a wall of claws and teeth and muscle. *Fight or freeze? Fight or freeze?* My breath halts. *Fight or—*

My boot lands on cloth, the wet fabric sliding against slippery stone. I barely register the flash of orange fur in the time it takes me to fall.

The pain of my hip hitting stone is nothing compared to the agony of the tiger's jaw clamping around my shoulder, his great teeth pressing deeply into muscle.

Pain explodes in my shoulder and I bite back a scream. Tye's tiger might let me live, but it is unlikely he'd extend the same courtesy to my males, should they come. Gathering all my strength, I try to kick the tiger off me instead, my foot hitting solid muscles.

Unimpressed, the tiger swings around and drags me away, my boots bouncing along the smooth stones. I raise my other arm and cling onto the fur of his neck, trying to take pressure off my shoulder. Between the pain and the tiger's thick limbs, glimpses of shoreline show us moving away from the river toward the mountain's darkness. Fire flares in my shoulder with each bump, until, several steps later, my head hits a stone and the world blinks away.

1 3

LERA

*C*onsciousness washes over me like a dream, my nose filling with the scents of mossy cave, animal fur, and blood. Cracking open my eyes, I see evening light shining beyond the opening, as warm and golden as before. I've not been out for long, then. Just enough for Tye's tiger to have dragged me to . . . wherever this is.

Pressing my hand to my screaming shoulder, I lift away my tunic collar. I don't know how, but he seems to have dragged me here without tearing or breaking anything too vital. Dark blue, purple, and red-tinged bruises bloom over my chest and collarbone and disappear around my shoulder.

Examination over, I slowly look around. The cave is about ten feet deep and tall enough for me to stand upright, if I could get to my feet. A pace away, Tye's tiger sits on his haunches and watches me.

"Is this your lair?" I mutter. "More to the point, am I here as your friend or your supper?"

The tiger opens his maw and roars again, that same wrong sound that I heard before. The one that shakes me to my core, especially now that it echoes from the walls, surrounding me with its force. Violence, yes, that's there, but mixed with something a great deal more frightening. Desire.

Not good. The fire in my shoulder banks itself to a nagging voice in the back of my mind while I race through my options. Reaching inside myself, I search for any spark of Tye's magic. Nothing. Tye's tiger doesn't engage magic the way his fae form does, and there's nothing for my body to mirror off of. Right. Slowly extending my good arm, I grope around for a good-sized stone, wrapping my fingers around the prize.

"Easy, Tye." I make my voice low and soothing, as if calming a skittish horse. Bringing my legs under me, I shift my weight onto my knees. "Just walking out now." When the tiger stays put, I dare to start rising.

Tye's tiger roars again, one front paw scratching the ground, a fevered blaze consuming his wide green eyes. My breath halts as the tiger stands, his hackles up, his dangling maleness heavy with readiness.

Icy terror crackles along my nerves, my heart pumping so hard and fast that my body shakes with each thump. When the tiger takes his first step toward me, I launch my stone at his head and bolt for the exit.

A wounded yelp squeezes my chest and I can't help halting. Turning. Feeling acid rise up my throat at the sight of blood soaking Tye's gorgeous fur, turning the white tufts of his ears pink and red. "Are you all right?"

The tiger swipes at me, his claws out and sharp.

Throwing myself out of the way, I pull out my knife, holding it between myself and the predator. My eyes sting, my throat choking on terror. *Mistake.* It was a mistake beyond reckoning to hesitate. The weapon in my hand trembles but stays.

Tye's tiger drops onto his elbows, his tail high in the air. His green eyes flash with need and pleasure. The predator likes the game. He knows exactly how he wants it to end. And with the next heartbeat, he pounces.

I feel the knife slide into muscle before the tiger's great force rips it from my hand. I fall flat on my back, the tiger's wide paws pinning me to the ground, his breath hot on my neck.

"No!" I scream with all the breath I have left. "No. Tye, stop! STOP."

The flash of light is so bright, it hurts my eyes. The weight atop me disappears at once, Tye's fae form rolling off me, his beautiful face a deadly shade of white. A patch of blood mats the hair just above his pointed ear, a larger patch soaking the breast of his green shirt, where the knife must have struck. Haunted green eyes find mine as he backs away, step by step, until he strikes the cave wall.

Relief washes over me so hard it leaves me dizzy.

"Tye," I gasp, pushing myself to a sitting position. Waiting for him to come to me.

Tye slides down the stone until his knees hit dirt. Hands curling like claws, he covers his face, letting his shoulder wound drip unhindered. "I'm sorry." His voice shakes, his fingers clutching his hair. "Stars. Stars. Stars." The words come under Tye's breath, each wilder and more desperate than the last. "What have I done? What have I done?"

"Tye." I crawl to him, pushing his hands away from his face until I can see his glistening eyes. "The tiger isn't you. I know that. It isn't your fault that you can't control him."

Tye snorts bitterly. "But it is, lass." Pulling free of my hold, he presses so hard against the wall that he looks like he's trying to escape into the stone. "Do you think you can make it back to the others? You shouldn't have to be around me."

"I'll make my own decisions." I sigh, strength seeping from me. I reach for his blood-soaked shirt and then stop. "If I cause you pain, is there a chance your tiger will return and maul me for it?"

"No." A whisper. The tears filling Tye's emerald eyes overflow, sliding silently down strong cheeks. His smattering of freckles, usually hidden, stand out against his pale skin. When I wipe them with the back of my hand, the male flinches away.

"Don't do that." I grip his uninjured shoulder. "Don't pull away from me. We've been through this with Shade's wolf—"

"This isn't like Shade," Tye says darkly.

"Explain." Ripping open his tunic, I examine the stab wound on his upper chest, right at the base of his shoulder. My own shoulder blazes in protest, but the pain feels like more of a general agony than the wrongness of true injury, thank the stars—or the tiger. The large cat meant to capture and mate, not kill.

"My tiger didn't try to mate with you. I did." Tye hisses in pain but holds rock-still. From the dark, slow bleeding, I think the blade missed any major arteries, though the sight of ripped-up flesh is enough to make my stomach churn. When I press a piece of wadded-up shirt against the puncture, the male's hands tighten against the stone wall. "I wanted you so badly that my needs slipped through the wall between the tiger and me. The animal felt my desire and acted on it to please me, even though I abandoned the beast centuries ago." Tye swallows, the effort to keep his eyes on me seeming to consume his body. Shame mars his perfect features, making tears burn in my throat. "And I had too little control over the beast to stop him."

I try to work through Tye's words but find only confusion. If the male truly wanted to couple with me, he wouldn't have rejected me time and time again. My jaw tightens. Tye chose a poor time for lies just now. I pull my hands back. "You are the one who's kept away from me."

"You deserve better than me, lass. I'm—" Tye stiffens, going from wounded to predatory in a heartbeat's time. "Someone is coming." Gaze focused on the cave entrance, he shoves me behind him.

"Lera!" Shade's voice calls a few moments before the shifter himself appears, frowning into the cave. He's shirtless and gleaming with sweat, steam practically rising off him in the swiftly cooling air. His tan, sculpted chest rises and falls with quick breaths. "Tye? I thought I heard a scream."

"Aye, you did." Tye's shoulders relax and he steps away, opening the line of sight between Shade and me. "Good thing, too. The lass is hurt."

"I can smell that." Shade's nostrils flare and I shudder at the thought of everything the male might be scenting. Blood, certainly. Tye's and mine both. Something more? Shade's jaw tightens. "How?"

"Me." Tye lifts his head, stepping closer to Shade. Baiting him to take a swing. To take me away.

"Stop it, Tye," I say.

The male ignores me. Takes another step closer to the entrance—to Shade's fists. "I hurt your mate, Shade."

My stomach tightens.

With visible effort, Shade takes a step back, one hand gripping the top of the cave. "You hurt her, you bastard? You fix it." The strain in the shifter's face calls to me, but when I start toward him, he shakes his head and pushes himself farther away. "Don't come any closer just now, cub. Please. I will . . ." The fingers of his free hand form a fist, which he thrusts into his pocket. "I will see you both tomorrow."

14

TYE

Tye stood frozen as Shade plodded away, all at once loving and despising his quint brother for trusting him with Lera. Of course, Shade didn't know the whole of what had happened, the truth that would give Tye nightmares for years to come. The worst part of it was that he remembered nothing of how it came to be. The last memory he could conjure was walking into the woods, the tiger inside him so desperate for freedom that Tye hadn't dared say goodbye to the lass. And then . . .

"No. Tye, stop! STOP." The tiger hadn't understood the words but somehow knew they were important. Felt it. And, overpowering his own instincts, the tiger yielded to Tye's fae form. He was a truly good tiger, a tiger who deserved a better partner than the ass he had.

Tye's cock had still been throbbing when he'd shifted and beheld the terrified female. With the next heartbeat, the realization of what he'd nearly done ripped open his soul.

"Upset that Shade wouldn't take me off your hands?"

Lera's voice pierced the cave's mossy air, the hurt in her chocolate eyes going beyond her bloodied clothes. Scratched and ruffled and unsteady, the lass still managed to look beautiful. Her long auburn hair tumbled loose over her shoulders, her soft lips pink from being bitten, her eyes large and dark against her pale face. Stars, between Lera's curves and personality alone, she was gorgeous no matter what she was doing.

Realizing that what Lera was doing presently was striding toward the cave exit, Tye stepped into her path. "You would have been safer and more comfortable with—"

"Where I'm comfortable is not for you to decide." Lera bumped Tye's injured shoulder with her own as she walked past. "I can accept a tiger's instincts. But you trying to bait Shade into ripping you to ribbons to avoid spending a night with me is a whole other matter."

"Lera!" Tye's throat tightened, the realization of how she'd taken the conversation just now penetrating his skull. Except now was minutes too late. The lass had already cleared the cave mouth and was currently picking her way up the trail that Shade had disappeared on not long ago. "Wait. Lera, that wasn't what I meant at all."

She quickened her pace.

A few more steps and there would be no turning back, Tye could feel it. And the very thought of losing his Lilac Girl sent terror racing along his spine. "Lera!" He ran after her, his long legs covering the distance easily. Once at her back, Tye tossed all wisdom and prudence to the wind and threw his arms around the lass, pulling her against him.

The soft warmth of her small form filled a bleeding void in his chest.

She elbowed him in the ribs. Hard. Bloody Coal and his bloody training.

"Let me go." Lera enunciated each word.

Tye turned her around, capturing her fury-filled gaze. "No." He lifted his chin. "Stars know there are a plethora of reasons for you to walk away from me, but this one isn't on the damn list. So either pick a better one or—"

Lera punched him. Right on his shoulder, sending knives of pain tearing through his left side. As she pulled back her hand for the next strike, Tye grabbed her wrist mid-motion, met her blazing gaze, and captured her mouth with his own, carnal need consuming his whole body.

Lera yanked her hand against Tye's restraining hold even as her mouth opened to his demand. The scent of her arousal struck him as hard as lightning, hardening him instantly, and the harder she fought, the more heavily her wet scent filled the air. Spurred on, Tye's tongue claimed Lera's mouth, plunging deep into her warmth to possess each inch, each fiber. This close, Tye felt the bounding beats of Lera's heart, his own drumming hard in harmony.

Pulling back, Tye gripped Lera's chin with his free hand, studying her face. The girl's lips were swollen from the kiss, the scents of arousal and fury, of need and hurt, all mixing together into a bouquet of *her*.

"I've been here before." The words Tye never wanted to say tumbled recklessly from his mouth. Leralynn could have any piece of his soul that she wished. And if she wanted none of it, Tye needed to know that too. "I injured my family, I injured my tiger, and now I've injured you. I asked Shade to take you because I'm infinitely better at creating problems than fixing them. And because . . ." He drew a breath, held it, and exhaled slowly before speaking. "Something is happening that I do not understand. Something I want to keep you safe from."

Lera studied him, her large, intelligent eyes piercing through his chest right to his heart. "What is happening?"

"My tiger is . . . rising, demanding more of my attention. He should have torn you apart, lass. I truly have no awareness of the beast. Or at least, I didn't until . . ." He brushed his thumb over her lips, savoring their softness. "Until you. Somehow, my tiger knew you were vital to me, felt it so strongly that he let *me* know. It was the first time we'd communicated at all since I tried to murder the beast in colthood."

Lera froze, her attention so focused on Tye that his heart stuttered. After a moment, her body softened, her willingness to grant Tye another chance as precious as a winter fire. "Tell me," she said quietly. "All of it. No lying or brushing me off this time, Tye."

Releasing her, he walked back to the cave, hearing her light steps behind him, and lowered himself to the floor. He held out his hand, a tourniquet around his heart easing when the lass took it. Allowed him to gather her close and savor the heat of her body as he confessed the truth to which he'd never given voice before. Not even to his quint brothers.

"The bond between a shifter's fae and animal forms is sacred, but it takes a great deal of time to develop, especially during the colt years. That is when the shifting matures from a blind instinct to a partnership."

"But yours never progressed beyond instinct," Lera said, her sweet voice vibrating against his chest. "Did something happen to you?"

Tye's body tightened, the question hitting the center of his heart. "No. Maybe if something had, all that followed would not be my fault. But no. Everything that happened was my own doing." He sighed, his heart racing even as he knew it was too late to retreat. "I wanted to train in flex. I had a talent for the sport, was drunk on the thrill of it. On the possibilities it could offer. My family is . . . well, the opposite of River's. My flex victories were going to change our fortune."

Tye closed his eyes, the cheering of phantom crowds filling his ears. "Once I set my mind on it, training became my entire world—and nothing that interfered with it could be permitted. Including the changes my body needed to make to mature." He swallowed, feeling words rise up his throat that he could never take back. "The first time I shifted, I missed practice because of that bloody tiger. And I knew it would get worse— that the animal would keep stealing my time, that the shifting would affect my finely tuned muscles and magic. The tiger threatened my future glory, and that meant war."

"A war on yourself?" Lera said.

Tye shrugged one shoulder. "On what my body was becoming. I couldn't be a shifter *and* a realm champion in flex. So I tried to sever the bond. Herbs, magics, anything and everything. Some of it effective, all of it dangerous. I failed to kill the tiger entirely, but I did a damn good job of mangling the bond beyond recognition. Retarding my body's changes long enough to win the championships. By the time I matured, I'd spent too little time in the feline form to even keep my own awareness."

Lera brushed her fingers over Tye's chest, hesitating on his pounding heart. He shivered lightly. "Did anyone else know?"

"My coaches, but they were willing to help me suppress my tiger. I was too bloody talented. When my family started to suspect . . . well, I learned to lie convincingly."

Lera frowned. "You do all that and then get drunk the

evening before the Realm Championship? That makes little sense."

A humorless chuckle escaped Tye's chest. "As the level at which I competed increased, so did the . . . incidents. A bought judge here, a faulty bar there. Unfortunately for my opponents, I could outperform them nonetheless. But when my path brought me head to head with the prince of Blaze, things escalated." Taking Lera's fingers, Tye brought them up to feel his brow, where an indent in the bone could still be felt beneath a small scar. "I received this by way of incentive to fumble a landing. Another time, a broken rib was a message to miss a target."

"So you started to lose?" she said softly. "To stay safe, you had to lose."

"No. I tried making noise about it, but my word meant nothing against the prince's. So I started to compete hurt. And I was bloody good enough to win still. The night before the Realm Championship . . . I wasn't home when the attack came. My mother and younger sister were. By the time the bastards were through with them, I'd gotten the message. The following day, I got so drunk to do what had to be done—to throw the competition—that I didn't even think of betting against myself. I think you know the rest."

"You missed the tournament, which the prince of Blaze proceeded to win," Lera said, her mind racing behind her gaze. "And you were in and out of jail cells until the quint call."

"There was rather little incentive to follow the rules at that point," Tye said simply. "And smuggling pays well." He swallowed painfully, unable to look at her for this part, to see in her eyes the moment she realized he'd been right to push her away. "Now do you see why I thought you should go with

Shade? If it were up to me, Lilac Girl, I would never let you out of my sight for the rest of my life. But it isn't up to me, especially now that you know the full truth. You deserve better, Lera. You deserve the world."

Silence trailed at the heels of Tye's words, the cave around them a capsule of secrets. Each memory shoving itself insistently from its hiding place in the depths of Tye's mind drove another needle into his soul. Fingers tightening on the rough stone, Tye inhaled the damp, mossy air and awaited judgment.

Several heartbeats passed before Lera rose to her knees, her cool hands gripping Tye's face. Tipping it to look so deeply into his eyes that Tye felt his soul bared beneath her intense chocolate gaze. Stars, if the girl could make him feel so vulnerable with one look, what could she do with a word? A step? Fear crackled along his veins, but when he tried to pull back, to escape for a bit of air, Lera would not let him.

"I see you, Tye." Her words rang gently through the cave, stopping Tye's heart. "And I want you. Not for play. I want you for *you*, forever."

Tye's blood stirred, waking him to Lera's words. She wanted him.

She wanted *him*.

The way he'd always longed for her but had been so certain she would never feel in return. He stared into her eyes, hardly daring to believe it.

"And I want forever to start now, Tye," she said quietly.

Blood roared in Tye's ears. Stars, he believed her. With every scrap of his soul. And every beat of his throbbing cock.

15

LERA

*M*y heart cracks at Tye's vulnerable gaze, the slow widening of his eyes as my words finally settle in his mind. My promise of wanting the true him finally melting the wall between us.

"Are you certain, Lilac Girl?" he asks, his voice strained as if he fears chasing off a mirage.

Leaning forward into his pine-and-citrus scent, I brush my lips gently over his. "Quite certain." A corner of my mouth quirks, my tongue tracing my teeth. "Though perhaps I should sample the merchandise first, given your criminal history and all."

Tye's face breaks into a dazzling white smile, his green eyes flashing with that feline mischief I've missed so, so much. "Oh, aye. But not here. The light's poor." Before I can even gasp, Tye snatches me to him and settles me on his hips as he rises, stepping from the cave into the soft evening light.

Along the shoreline, the river rushes along, its surface equal parts sparkling and treacherous. With the setting sun, the horizon is starting to shimmer with bright orange hues, the *kraa-kraa* of white birds circling overhead a harmony to the roaring water.

Tye stops mid-step, his attention rapt on the birds. "There's a memory tickling the back of my mind. Not an image, but a sensation." A hint of a smile touches his face. "I remember wanting to leap into the sky and catch that bird between my teeth."

"Your tiger wanted to eat a bird?" I ask. "Or just catch it?"

"Neither. He wanted to bring it to someone very important." Tye's ears color. "Did I by chance—"

"A rabbit. A hare. A deer. Don't get me started. Wait. You said the tiger wasn't trying to mate with me—why bother with the offerings?"

"I think he's giving me another chance," Tye whispers, a tiny, glistening drop beading at the corner of his eye. "He thinks you are worth it."

"And that *you* are." I wrap my arms around Tye's neck, my brows furrowing. "Though I'm not sure what to think about a seven-hundred-pound busy-body tiger playing matchmaker. Where are we going anyway?"

Tye points his chin at the river, where a circle of stones forms a basin several paces from the shore. The water inside the stones lies stiller than its rushing brethren, suggesting some isolation from the main river's currents—but certainly not from its temperature.

"I think the tiger got the brains of the duo. At least he brought me to a nice dry cave," I say, waiting for clarification. When Tye strides into the water instead, I shriek, digging my heels into his backside to find purchase higher on his body. "Not. Funny." My words escape lungs that are already seizing with the cold. I start struggling to get away from the male but then think better of it. If I got down now, the water would only come up higher on me. "I'm going to kill you. Kill, kill, kill."

Tye chuckles, cringing slightly as a rogue wave soaks him further. The warrior's wet clothes cling to his muscles, showing off lithe lines that bend and flex with every controlled shift of weight. A tiger made fae. I bury my face in Tye's neck, inhaling his clean, male scent. Heat from his body roars into mine despite the wetness, as his confident steps brave the waves all the way to the little circle of stones.

I feel Tye's magic wake the instant we step into the basin, his hand skimming the surface of the water. Power ripples from his core, gradual and controlled, until the first wisps of steam rise into the air, the water slowly giving way to Tye's touch. Taking a deep, cautious breath, I inhale the warm fumes and taste the hint of seaweed rising with the steam. A moan escapes me as I borrow my face deeper into Tye's shoulder.

A sudden, delicious hardness presses back against me in answer.

Finding a ledge, Tye lowers me into the exquisitely warm water, the stones dutifully protecting the oasis from the splashing cold beyond. I shimmy to settle lower in the—

A sharp pain scatters my pleasure and I flinch, clamping my palm over the livid bruises on my shoulder. *Deep breath.* I repeat the instruction to myself in hopes of my lungs obeying, while the wakened flesh screams its protest.

Crouching in front of me, Tye strokes my hair. "I know it hurts," he whispers, making no motion to cover his own stab wound. "Let me see the damage."

"I'm all right." I swallow, trying to hide the pain.

"Aye, well, I was planning on taking your shirt off either

way." He smiles roguishly, but his emerald eyes betray his worry. Without waiting for a response, the male reaches forward to unbutton my tunic, working the silver clasps apart one by one. If his shoulder screams at him for it, none of it shows in the strong lines of his focused face. His mussed hair stands up in fiery tufts, and I run my good hand through it as he works, making his breath come slightly faster.

Click. Click. Click.

My own breath stalls as Tye opens the last clasp and pushes the wet fabric off my shoulders, pressing a kiss to a scratch at the base of my collarbone, the side of my neck, the top of my ribs. His hands slide down my arms, massaging the aching muscles until I remember how to breathe. When my body finally relaxes beneath his gentle touch, Tye unwinds my chest wrap to let my breasts tumble free against the burbling water.

Cupping a breast in each hand, slowly, almost reverently, Tye looks into my eyes, his own burning with intensity. So different from the other times he's touched me.

I'm breathless, almost nervous. After wanting him for so long, I'm still marveling at the realization that Tye has wanted me too. All this time. That it was the depth—not lack—of his feelings for me that kept the male away.

"May I take your mind off the pain?" he asks, his thumbs brushing along my peaked nipples.

Zings of sensation shoot from my breasts all the way to my toes. I swallow, my mouth suddenly dry despite the salt water and the steam. My mind fights for clarity against the insistent throbbing in my sex and loses.

"Was that a yes?" Tye murmurs.

"What was the question?"

"This." Tye's lips descend upon mine, his tongue deftly

slipping into my mouth and coaxing my own into a deep, consuming kiss that has me moaning against his mouth. His scent surrounds me, his delicious taste and warm lips. With the next heartbeat, the male's hand slides to tangle in my hair, his grip tightening to the edge of pain, which somehow magnifies the pleasure of his thumb stroking my nipple. I can't move, as if held in shackles by some new brand of magic, unable to think beyond my growing need.

I melt into Tye, my hips pressing forward in search of his hardness. My mind numbing to all thought but the gripping tension coiling through my body. I rake my hand across Tye's muscled back and he growls, his kiss deepening with voracious hunger. His tongue rolls over mine, no longer sweet or playful but carnal enough to wake each of my nerves. To steal my breath.

This time, when Tye releases me, my swollen lips tingling from the loss of his, I'm so engulfed in the haze of his essence that Tye grips my shoulders just to keep me from toppling over. Stars. The things this male can do with a kiss alone . . .

I shake myself back to reality. Rub my face. Inhale the mix of cold air and warm steam. Forcing my mind beyond my throbbing sex takes more effort than any sparring match with Coal, but once I manage, I remember where we are. How we got here.

"Your shoulder." I reach out to stroke Tye's arm. The cut beside his clavicle looks clean, but his tightly coiled muscles and the memory of my blade slicing into flesh speak the truth. I let the male *carry* me here. "You are hurt."

Tye barely seems to hear me, his intense eyes glazed with the same need that throbs inside me. "Mmm. I forgot about that."

"Liar."

Instead of answering, Tye lifts me to my feet and makes efficient work of ridding me of my trousers. His own follow a moment later, and as much as I'd like to help, I can't take my eyes off the efficiency of his motions, the way his body engages only the muscles it must and not a single fiber more.

"Not a liar," Tye murmurs into my ear, his soft breath warm and tickling. "A male. One with something else on his mind."

And not only on his mind, I note from the hardness bumping against me, its velvety head impossibly large and opinionated.

"Can I touch you?" I ask, cringing at the awkwardness of my own words.

Instead of laughing, Tye turns us around and sits on my old underwater ledge. His shaft full and high, he lifts me by my hips and settles me carefully atop him. With my opening just over his cock, I feel every full inch of him as I slide down, my tightness stretching to accommodate his size. I moan and Tye's eyes shudder in response. The male's strong hands dig into my hips, guiding them, controlling the impaling descent. An inch. Two. Three. The fullness inside me throbs and I clench around him, even as I know there is more. More than I can possibly take inside.

16

LERA

*W*hen I let out a shaky breath, Tye's finger opens my folds and traces the sensitive tissues around my apex, teasing the hood with leisurely strokes that send spasms along my thighs.

His fullness throbs, stretching me so insistently that I whimper as the head of his cock conquers every ridge inside me, sending a new wave of need with each *bump, bump, bump.* When my weight finally settles on Tye's lap, his cock alive and pulsing, my breath catches.

For a moment, our gazes meet and hold. I notice new specks of silver in Tye's brilliant green eyes, new freckles across his cheekbones. A tiny scar over his lip that I pull into my mouth, eliciting a soft growl in his chest.

Tye's chest rises and falls with rapid breaths as he slides his hands from my hips to my breasts, trapping them in his large, callused palms. His thumbs stroke my sensitive nipples before his mouth closes over the left one, suckling it to a hard point.

When I gasp, Tye adds a nip to his assault before attending similarly to my right breast, stoking the fire in my core until it is nearly impossible to bear.

With a growl, I surge against him. Again. Harder. The need to feel the length of him along my channel is so strong that it hurts, the ache spreading all the way to my fingertips. Cursing Tye under my breath, I slide along him with increasing speed, savoring his fullness inside me. My breath quickens, the wet and swollen tissues around my entry rippling in rhythm to Tye's pulsing cock as I undulate with the lapping waves.

I brace myself on Tye's shoulders, the male gripping one of my hips to help, lifting and lowering me with growing urgency. His other hand replaces his mouth on my breast, his fingers flicking my nipple to the rhythm of our thrusts. In the sinking light, Tye's biceps bulge, his green eyes gleaming. Too much. The sight and feel of him. With a sudden surge, I claim his mouth, a clash of teeth and tongues.

More, more, more, my body demands, the steam rising from the water filling my lungs as absolutely as Tye's cock fills my sex.

Yet, instead of satisfying my cravings, each pump along Tye's shaft only flares the desire inside me. I moan in frustration and overwhelming heat. The muscles of my thighs quiver, zings of sensation shooting across my skin.

A predatory satisfaction sparkles through the wild lust in Tye's green eyes. The bastard knows exactly what he is doing to me with those hands. With that mouth.

Two can play this game, tiger. Grabbing Tye's hair, I force his head to the side.

The male startles but allows me to expose his neck.

Baring my teeth, I sink them into his skin and—

Tye is on his feet with a growl before I can conquer him, the blazing inferno in his eyes now echoing the predator he is.

"I think I'm through allowing my food to play with me," he rumbles, lowering me to my feet. Shoving me to the other side of the basin, the male lays me down on the smooth lip, using his elbows to move my thighs apart. Steam so hot it is just short of painful rushes in to explore my exposed sex and opened backside. When a tiny spark of fire bites just above my roused bud, I scream, my hips jerking against the sensation, clenching against the nothingness inside.

Tye's strong hand presses into my hip, keeping me down. Pinned. A second tiny spark nips the other side of the hood. Then the top.

"You . . . are using . . . magic." My accusation comes in pants, burning need racking my body with each savage strike of my heart.

"Aye, I am." Tye rubs my inner thighs, the soothing motion at utter odds with the havoc he's unleashing above. "Magic is as much a part of me as my blood. But I've other parts too, lass."

Hoisting one of my legs atop his shoulder, the male reaches between my legs to stroke my wet folds. A moment later, his finger slides inside me. A second finger. A third. Each increase mirrored by the same number of sparks teasing my bud. The edge of pain wakes my every nerve, magnifies each sensation to unbearable sharpness.

I writhe uncontrollably, pressing against Tye's fingers, which refuse to move any faster. When the head of his cock replaces them at my opening, I'm ready to weep with the promise of coming release. With a sharp thrust, Tye plunges into me, the sensation so searing that I nearly topple over the edge then and there.

Except . . . except there is a sudden slickness circling my other opening and I freeze, recognizing the sensation.

My body writhes in rebellion, stopping at once when Tye's sparks nip the most sensitive, swollen part of my apex in penalty. The instant I still, the finger at my bottom slides in.

My muscles spasm over the dual fullness inside me. Tye's cock, still until now, thrusts deeply to strike the sensitive spot inside. In my bottom, his finger echoes his cock, thrusting in and out in perfect contrast. The seesaw of sensation would have me bucking up a storm if Tye's free hand wasn't holding me down firmly. Making me able to do nothing but feel *him*.

Thrust. Thrust. Thrust. Each plunge sends a new shock of need through my belly, the backs of my legs, my toes. Each wet slap sounds deafeningly loud amidst the low rumble of the river and occasional cries of birds. Tye's beautiful face is tight with concentration, fending off his own release in order to draw out mine. Gasping, I lick salty drops of river spray from my lips. *Thrust. Thrust. Thrust.*

When the tiny sparks circle my apex again, stalking closer and closer like a tiger's pointed claws, the abyss I've been waiting for opens itself before me.

"Tye!" I choke on my desperation, knowing I can't hold on for another second more and yet feeling a deeper need unfurl inside my soul. "I want to be closer to you."

Tye hesitates for only a moment. Disengaging, he pulls my legs around his waist and stands, sheathing himself back inside me with a single, well-aimed stroke. I lock my ankles over his backside, my arms around his neck. The cool air swirls over our naked skin. The male's green eyes are fevered with the same want that crushes my core.

I hold his eyes, our faces only an inch apart. "I love you, Tye."

Taking my mouth with his and thrusting again, even deeper, Tye releases his magic along my sex until it pinches my bud in a tidal wave of ecstasy.

"Stars, I love you," he gasps, the words sending us both over the edge.

WE RETURN to the cave to discover that someone—likely Shade, given the presence of a jar of green salve that makes Tye cringe on sight—has left us a bundle of supplies and food. Leaving our clothes outside to dry, we huddle together naked atop a cloak, Tye's carefully built fire warming the space. Fatigue and contentment wash over me like waves lapping at the rocks.

"Can we keep the flames burning all night?" I ask, my eyes heavy. With full darkness now blanketing the mountains, the temperature is low enough to make my breath mist.

"It wouldn't be safe, Lilac Girl." Tye kisses the top of my head. "Not with so much wind and dry brush around. But I can do a bit of something." Pulling a few fist-sized stones together, Tye lays his hands over them. When he tucks the rocks beneath the cloak a few minutes later, warmth seeps through the cloth. Grinning at my happy sigh, Tye snuffs out the fire, pulls me against him, and whispers for us to sleep.

I close my eyes, feeling the world fall away for a time. But not long enough. The night is so cold that even Tye's arms around me aren't enough to ward off the chill, and once the stones cool, I dare not ask Tye to warm them again. Between his injuries and heating the pool, even I know the male has used too much magic already.

Keeping my eyes closed, I let fatigue and the frigid mountain night battle each other in silence. Eventually, somehow, I drift off into a warm sleep that smells very much of a tiger's thick fur cocooning my body.

17

LERA

For just under two weeks, we trek through the mountains and plains of the neutral lands, and then the rolling, forested hills of Slait, the days long and increasingly tense. River alternates between outlining and re-outlining our plans—all of which boil down to luring Griorgi to the palace—and long, stony silences that not even Tye's improved humor can shatter. Tye has been shifting form more often since our coupling—since sharing the truth of his past with me and giving me leave to brief the rest of the quint on what happened. The glimpses of true humor returning slowly to Tye's eyes, especially when they meet my own, are the best part of the cold journey. The only good part of the damn journey.

The nights are so cold that I have to lie next to the fire (when we're allowed one), under my bedroll, and pressed between two males just to fall asleep. River and Shade. Shade and Tye. Tye and River. Never Coal. As if lying beside me will only kindle inevitable disaster.

Though Coal trains me in swordplay still—pulling me from my saddle at lunch break or before dawn or whatever other terrible time he can seize upon to make me miserable— the shield he's locked around himself, around the strange magic connecting us, grows more impenetrable each day. As if the male is training himself to shut me out. The only times I can feel Coal's purple strands of power are when River oversees my echo practice. In a clearing, on a rippling hilltop over a bustling Slait town, on a vast rocky slope—that last one nearly resulting in an avalanche.

"Can you tell Coal that you take back that reprimand over our kiss?" I finally ask Shade, after we've cleared up breakfast on what River promises to be the last day of the trek. The other males are already mounted and ready to ride, Sprite prancing unhappily at the wolf shifter's proximity. I pat the mare's neck soothingly. "Tell him that one unwise choice of when to share his magic isn't cause for two weeks of brooding."

Shade rocks back on his heels, his voice low enough for my ears alone. "Why would I wish to do that?"

I frown at him, my mind scrambling through my memories for something I might have missed. "Why wouldn't you?"

"I rarely give orders, cub," Shade says, his yellow eyes piercing mine. Not the impertinent lupine or kind male I'm used to, but River's second-in-command. Steel beneath velvet. "When I do, I expect them to be followed. And when it comes to safety—your safety most of all—I've little desire to toy about."

"Shade—"

He shakes his head, cutting off my words. "I'm aware that Coal fears his magic hurting you. He miscalculated pushing you in the arena. Failed to consider what would happen in the bedchamber, which left you with broken ribs—"

"That was my fault. I pushed him—"

"And ignored the consequences of offering magic against a healer's orders. I'm all right with him feeling a bit of the sting from it." Shade's finger catches my chin before I can turn away, the power of his presence rolling over me in a great wave. His tone turns gentle, but not weak. "And I'm all right with you feeling the sting too, cub. There were two of you sharing that kiss, sharing the bed before that. I don't imagine you like seeing Coal in pain any more than he enjoys seeing you in it. But if you want to mend what's broken, you'll need to do it yourselves. I stand by my earlier decision."

Shade kisses the top of my head and shifts into wolf form, leaving me nothing to do but climb onto Sprite's back.

The phantom touch of his lips and words stays with me well into the afternoon, when the sight of Slait Palace's soaring marble towers rising majestically over the horizon sends a wave of relief through me. A sentiment that is not shared by all, if Coal pulling his stallion further and further toward the back of our procession is any indication.

"Is there any destination at which you actually enjoy arriving?" I ask, maneuvering Sprite beside the male.

"A battlefield," he says, his voice as dark as his clothes. With his hair pulled back into a tight bun and a sword hilt rising above each shoulder, Coal certainly looks more prepared to walk onto a killing ground than the palace's plush carpeting. "What are you so bloody happy about?"

"Bed. Bath. Vegetables." I count the amenities on my fingers.

Coal's face remains impassive.

When I reach out to touch his forearm, he shifts his weight, nudging the horse away.

My jaw tightens. "Coal—"

"Leralynn!" River calls from the front of the column, his hand held out to me, gray eyes unreadable.

"Go." Coal jerks his chin forward before circling Czar around to put even more distance between us.

Suppressing a frown, I nudge Sprite into a slow canter to see what River is about. Sitting comfortably atop his stallion, River looks every inch the commander and prince. His rich blue coat is somehow both clean and unrumpled, his knee-high leather boots shining in the sun. If the cold wind ruffling his short brown hair nips at him the way it does me, River lets none of the discomfort show. When I rein up beside him and reach for his outstretched hand, he leans down from his horse and shamelessly plucks me from my saddle.

Ignoring sounds of protest from both Sprite and me, River settles me in front of him, his powerful thighs and torso bracketing me on three sides. "The last time we came to Slait, someone stole you away. This time, I'm taking precautions."

"Aye, except those precautions are going to start aching any moment now," Tye says, grabbing hold of my mare's dropped reins as I register that River's hardness does, in fact, press against my backside.

My face heats but River just wraps his arms around my waist and kicks his stallion into a canter that has me gripping the saddle horn for dear life. "Don't let Coal see you doing that." River's voice is barely audible over the wind, his horse taking the wide dirt road in a smooth run. "Holding the saddle throws off your balance."

"Riding double at a neck-breaking gait throws off *me*."

River snorts but his arms tighten further around me as we

ride into the outskirts of the clean, sprawling capital city, with its ordered white buildings and gaudy fountains, surrounded by rippling lawns and winter flowers. Rich curtains drape nearly every window, the bursting flowerpots hung outside coordinated by color. Townspeople bow formally as we pass, and River, even in his haste, lifts a friendly hand in return salute, drawing out warm smiles from the otherwise reserved fae.

Several of the children shyly sneak strips of meat from their pockets, tempting Shade's wolf to trot over on his silent paws. All blissfully unaware of why we are here, of the silent battle for the throne that we are about to unleash.

"I hope Shade gets a stomachache," I mutter, watching the gray wolf sprawl shamelessly before several young girls, all eager to scratch his furry belly and ears while sneaking more and more treats from pockets and pouches.

"Oh, he will," River assures me, steering us up the cobblestone path that winds toward the palace. Since Autumn brought me in through a Gloom fold on my first visit, this is my first time approaching the palace gates, and their beauty takes my breath. River slows in front of them, letting me take in the elaborately carved iron, inlaid with gold reliefs and opaque blue stones that match the color of Slait's flag, whipping in the wind from the tallest tower. "As I was saying, the last time we came, Autumn spoiled the approach. This time, you can enjoy the full experience."

I open my mouth to point out that it's River, not Autumn, whom I hold responsible for the disaster of my debut visit to the palace—thanks to him keeping the truth about his royal heritage from me—but the tension in River's body pauses my retort. Light words aside, River is returning home not as a son or prince, but as a challenger to the

117

throne he's never wanted. I rest my palm over his hardened knuckles and he squeezes me tighter to him, dropping a kiss on my ear.

"How long do you think it will be before Griorgi comes?" I ask. Autumn's network of patrols reported that the king has stayed away from the palace since the confrontation in Karnish, but not even they know all the folds in the Gloom that Griorgi has surely built. I hope we were out and about in the countryside long enough for the king to have gotten River's message. "Could he have gone into hiding?"

"Griorgi doesn't hide, he schemes." Tye trots up to us, my mare's reins in one hand. "We—" Tye cuts off as two dozen armed warriors step through rippling air from the Gloom, swords and bows already drawn. A wall of Slait's navy blue and gold, sunlight glinting off metal.

Staring at an impossibly large arrowhead pointed at my chest, my heart jumps into a sprint. The wind hitting my face suddenly feels hot, the world suffocatingly small. Two dozen armed warriors against us five. My thighs grip the horse beneath me, the sensitive stallion dancing until River's calm hand on the reins soothes him.

"You have a dangerous sense of humor, Sparkle," Tye calls, throwing back his head. "Put away your toys before Coal breaks them."

A wave of relief softens my spine as the air ripples again, this time welcoming Autumn, stunning in a shimmering gray gown with strands of matching silk woven into her crown of braids. Being back home, with the full extent of her wardrobe, clearly suits her. Walking through the parting sea of warriors, my friend grins at me for a second—taking another second to examine my torn, stained, road-weary outfit with a dark look and an audible sigh—before weighing River with her gray gaze. "Is it too much to hope that you froze something off in those mountains?"

"What's with the display?" River waves his hand over the small army, who are just now condescending to lower their weapons. "Showing off?"

Autumn gives River a dark look. "I wish. Kora is more paranoid here than Tye is around too many guards. She's having patrols shadow everyone approaching the palace."

"Indeed." River swings himself out of the saddle then lifts me down to stand beside him. He surveys the warriors a final time before settling on Kora, whose shoulders stiffen. River nods to her. "Thank you for keeping Autumn safe. Her and us."

Kora brings her fist to her heart. "We've searched the palace for evidence of Griorgi's activity and found nothing, sir. No communications or magical traces. He wasn't working out of here to set up that portal."

"No, I don't imagine he would have been." Handing the horse off to one of the guardsmen, River puts a guiding hand in the small of my back and falls in step beside Autumn and Kora. "He wouldn't wish to give Jawrar the key to Slait, hence the setup in Karnish—however much of the town is still left." The male squeezes my shoulder and turns to his sister. "Any new theories on why Griorgi tried to bring me over to his side? I don't have Father pegged as sentimental."

"Agreed. You need a conscience for sentimentality." Autumn pulls a journal out of a satchel across her shoulder and flips through the dogeared pages. "I've been working through that one for a while. Most likely . . ." She frowns at her notes and trails off, the silence shifting slowly from expectant to pregnant.

"Autumn?" River prompts.

119

"Mmm?"

River gives a short growl.

Kora's blue eyes actually dare to flash at the male, who just points at his sister in exasperation.

"She's not slept more than four hours a night since we left." Kora brushes her hand along Autumn's forearm, waiting until the smaller female looks up at her before asking, more gently than River did, "What were you going to say about King Griorgi?"

"Oh. Jawrar and Griorgi talked about wanting me as well, right?" Autumn leafs back in her journal. "Some silliness about wanting my assistance in handling Slait's Gloom patrols."

"Given that the Gloom patrols have answered to you for several hundred years now, it seemed a logical proposition," River says.

"Logical sounding, certainly. But Griorgi would never trust an army that he doesn't control directly." Autumn taps a line of text. "I think Father is misdirecting Jawrar as to the reason he wants River and me. And when we take out sentiment, the only connection remaining between the three of us is blood."

A shiver runs through me, resonating with the tension saturating the air. Where I'd thought to find creature comforts, the Slait Palace feels more like the battleground that Coal sought. Even without the enemy here, the war has already begun. The dread that I'd managed to avoid during our long journey now seeps into my blood, similar to what I used to feel when I labored in Zake's stable—when, despite the sweet scent of hay and horse and emptiness, I knew the estate's master *would* come. And so would a beating. I force my voice to be steady. "What does blood have to do with it?"

"When it comes to the ancient magics that Griorgi is

toying with, there are few things more powerful than blood—especially the magic-filled blood of our line," Autumn says. "Don't forget, most fae can't even step into the Gloom. I think Griorgi used his own blood to open the portal in Karnish—it's the only substance with enough power and allegiance to him to crack the wall between Mors and Lunos. And I think he'll need much more blood than he can spare next time, when he'll try to make a crack large enough to bring an army through."

18

LERA

*A*utumn's words hang in the air, making bumps race like ants along my skin long after she excuses herself back to the library and the patrol melts silently back to their posts in the Gloom. Coal peels away the moment we enter the palace courtyard, which looks very much like when we last left, with its vibrant flowerbeds and castle domes stretching up to the brilliant blue sky. Except there is a different feel to the air now. A sulfur-like tension that hums with invisible danger.

And yet, despite the deadly confrontation with Griorgi crawling over the darkening horizon, seeing Coal duck alone into the stable twists my chest. Shade's words return to me, an echo of the ones he'd uttered to Tye. In essence: You broke it, you fix it.

Waving away the hostler who appears to take charge of the horses, I collect Sprite and the remaining two stallions and head for the stable myself. Pulling open the barn door, which slides easily along well-oiled rails, I inhale the comforting smells. The mixture of grain and straw and horse sweat.

Warm and welcoming. With the evening in full swing, the hostlers are gone, having left behind filled water buckets, clean stalls, and fresh hay.

Coal, as expected, is here still, brushing down Czar's already shining coat. I watch the male, the muscles bunching beneath his leather vest as he moves the coarse brush. Beside Coal, Czar looks like a normal-sized horse, though no sane being would think such of the stallion. I cringe at the memory of thinking I could ride the beast. And then at another memory, the time I shared Coal's saddle, his warm, strong body supporting mine. His cock growing stiff against my backside.

Where did *that* male go?

River's stallion gives a neigh of displeasure at being kept waiting.

Coal turns, his blue eyes heart-stoppingly bright. "Mortal?" The cautious note in his voice is intoxicating. Frowning at River's now dancing stallion, the male strides up and takes the reins from me, staring down the heady horse before walking him to a stall. When the warrior returns for Tye's mount, his leathery male musk makes my thighs clench together. Letting the horse into a corner pen, Coal pauses, his back still to me. "Is there a reason you are here?"

"No." Suddenly unable to hold still, I let Sprite into a stall, leaving on her halter but unclipping the lead rope from the headstall. "Yes."

Coal turns, cocking an annoyed brow.

Striding across the barn, I reach around the male's neck, my heart pattering as I pull his mouth down toward mine. The taste of him fills me before we even touch, metallic and powerful and very male. I brace for the feel of his hard lips and—

Nothing.

Coal pulls back before we can connect, one strong hand sliding across my arm to unhook it from behind his head.

No matter how I've braced myself for it, the sting of rejection hurts enough to close my throat outright. "Bastard." I hurl the word with all my might, jerking my hand away altogether. "Was it just a game to you? Or a bloody tool to share magic? Plainly not something worth fighting for after a single mistake."

Coal catches my wrist again, his grip tight. "Not a *single* mistake, mortal. When it comes to allowing you to echo my magic, not even my decisions are sound. As for indulging in lust—when I think with my cock instead of my head—in case you've forgotten, the last time I let that happen, you had broken ribs and worse to show for it. I bloody *kissed* you as we left the Citadel and even that cost more than it gave. Some things are not meant to be. We wager enough going against Griorgi and his hordes of Mors nightmares without your risking a punctured lung just to satisfy my cock."

"That isn't fair."

"If you are looking for a fair life, stars' blessings to you," Coal growls, the edges of his stunning face shadowed in the filtered light. "Damn it, Lera. When I work you in the sparring ring, I know exactly where each of my blows will land, how deep each bruise will go. You might exit a sparring ring hurting all over, but you'll never walk out truly injured. I can't make the same promise with my magic. Not even when I'm in full control. If I don't keep myself in check, you can see my damn nightmares, feel them as your own—let alone do damage to your body. I don't know what is safe." He enunciates the last words as if speaking to a child. "I don't know what is right. I. Don't. Know."

"You don't know?" My chest heaves, the blood rushing through my head so loud I can barely hear my own thoughts. How dare the bastard make this his decision alone? Decide for us both what my body needs. Wants. Deserves. "Is that it?" I ask coolly. "You don't know all the cosmic truths of the universe, and your fear of injuring me is the only reason you've turned into a bloody monk?"

"I think it's enough of one, don't you?"

I twist my hand to pit all my strength against Coal's thumb and, slipping free, cross my arms over my chest. "Fine." I raise my chin, meeting Coal's piercing blue gaze. "Then I have a better idea. How about you not injure me?"

Coal slams the heel of his hand into a wooden post mere inches from my head. "You think it's that simple? My body—"

"I don't intend to give your body a choice in the matter," I snap into his face, my pulse racing. Lifting up the lead rope I hold in my hand, I let the thick restraint dangle in the space between us. "Since you are of the opinion that denying a body what it wants for some higher moral purpose is a good idea, then let's go with it. Except I think I prefer that we deny the choice to your body, not mine."

Coal's gaze seizes on the rope, every muscle in him going rigid. In the intimate light of the setting sun and carefully hung lanterns, the male's shadow spreads like a pair of wings over the floor. His powerful chest rises and falls in such an even rhythm that I know he's working to control it. "What *exactly* do you mean?"

Rising on my toes, I run a finger over Coal's lips. "You fear injuring me. So I will make certain you can't."

Coal's face pales. "You want to restrain me."

"Yes. And yes, it will scare the stars out of you. Out of me too. But I'm asking you to trust me, and I don't *know* whether

I'm pushing you more than you can bear. There is no text in Autumn's library that spells out how our two bodies and magics and souls work together. So we figure it out, and we make mistakes if we have to. And it might not happen in one night. Or one week. Or one tumble in the sheets." I put my hand on his chest, his heart pounding against my palm. "You fear losing control so I'm removing that option until you are ready to risk it. And when you are, I will trust you to try. As I'm asking you to trust me now." A corner of my mouth quirks. "You might actually enjoy what I have in mind."

"I highly doubt it," Coal mutters, a note of surrender in his voice.

19

LERA

I squeeze Coal's shoulder and step away to lock the latches on both entrances. When I return, he's standing right where I left him. I hold out my hand. Palm up. "Give me your wrist."

The muscles of Coal's jaw tighten, rippling the skin along his face, but he doesn't step away this time. Under his fear, his wild eyes, I can see it—the very beginnings of curiosity. Arousal.

"I won't hurt you," I say quietly, my hand opening and closing in a *give me* gesture. "And I won't let you hurt me. But you have to trust that."

With strained slowness, Coal's heavy wrist settles into my palm, his pulse bounding so hard that I can feel it thumping beneath his skin. Before the male can change his mind, I guide him to the very post he struck earlier and loop the rope through one of the metal rings anchored high up into it. Moving slowly enough to keep from startling him, I secure

Coal's wrists to the hanging rope ends, letting him test the restraints when I finish my knots.

"Can you get out?" I ask.

Coal assesses the rope and beam above. "I could snap the wood, but it would take a bit of work."

"You can't snap the wood, Coal. The post is as thick as my palm."

His jaw flexes. "I'm aware. The qoru—"

"I'm not the qoru." Taking the male's face between my palms, I pierce his eyes with mine. "You can get free just by asking me to release you. No violence required. All right?" I wink at him. "Unless you suddenly feel like it, of course."

Coal swallows. Nods. Inhales sharply as I let my hands roam over his body, letting all my instincts free, my longing to touch his perfect, battle-hardened muscles to my heart's content. I spread my palms along the great bulk of his pectorals before moving to the laces of his shirt. The thin cords make a whooshing sound as I pull each free and drop them onto the carefully swept floor.

The heat coming off the male is strong enough to bake bread, and the tension in his muscles as he struggles to stay still beneath my touch is as heartbreaking as it is exciting. With the shirt opened, the top of Coal's sculpted abdomen is visible through the bottom corner. Of course, with his hands bound, I realize I can't get the bloody thing over his head no matter how many laces I undo.

The corner of Coal's mouth twitches as he comes to the same realization. Though he probably worked that out for himself minutes ago.

I meet his blue eyes, the heat in mine making him lean back warily. "I hope this isn't one of your favorites." Running my hands along Coal's waist, hips, and thighs, I bend down to pull a knife from his boot.

The male stills.

Putting the sharp blade against the fabric, I cut through it with quick, jerky motions that have the cloth sliding off his smoothly muscled frame, his breath hitching at the blade's nearness. Placing the knife within reach, I crouch again to relieve Coal of his left boot, then his right. By the time I start on his fly, what was left of color in the warrior's face is gone, his eyes watching every single one of my movements as his heart pounds.

"It's me, Coal," I whisper into his ear, though I have to stand on tiptoes to do so. "It's you and me. And no one else but the magic we'll release."

Hooking my thumbs into the waistband of his trousers, I slide them off his muscular legs. His cock twitches as its restraints disappear and chill air brushes bare skin. I mean to study Coal's face but my eyes trip on the large shaft, standing even now, as arousal battles fear. When I run my hand over it, tracing the full veins along its sensitive underside, the whole damn thing wakens even further, Coal's body going rigid against the post.

Looking up, I find the male's chest heaving, the muscles of his jaw so tight that they quiver beneath his skin. My own heart speeds, the fear rolling off Coal so palpable that my pulse responds in a sympathetic gallop. I brush his cock again, this time watching his eyes. Knowing there is more lurking underneath.

I feel it a moment later, the rumbling of magic waking in my chest, an answering call to the power roaring in Coal. The first magic I've felt from him in two weeks, outside of River's cautious training sessions. Yes. "Do you want me to stop?" I ask.

He shakes his head no.

"Good," I whisper. "Neither do I." I brush my hands over his muscles, assessing. Deciding. My mouth aches to close around that standing cock of his, but I rein myself in. Hard. Licking one of Coal's nipples instead, I feel him jerk against the restraints—this time with more need than fear. I attend to his other nipple next, circling it with my tongue before taking the whole of it in my mouth. Showing Coal my plans for lower down.

He gasps, his cock full and throbbing against me. "You'll pay for this in the sparring ring, mortal."

"Mmm." My hands roam over the hard squares of his abdomen, each fitting like a brick in my palm. My fingers slide lower and lower along the grooves, my mouth watering at the smooth skin covering steel strength. Reaching the top of his tight blond curls, I feel the wetness of my own sex seeping into my underthings.

One hand cupping Coal's sack, I use my foot to spread his legs apart, my motions hard and ruthless.

Coal curses, his hips bucking in spite of himself as I stroke his cock with my tongue, running the tip along his whole luxurious length. Up and down, up and down, stopping only to rub around the throbbing head.

A bead of moisture forms along Coal's slit and I lap it up, the salty taste of him making my sex ache with the need to have him inside me. The simmering magic in my blood blazes. Roars. Demands a fight, a match, a release strong enough to explode the skies.

I nip Coal, the magic inside me—Coal's magic—wanting so, so much more.

Taking him deeply into my mouth, I suck the throbbing shaft, my hands sliding in rhythm along his sensitive skin. Again. Again. My mouth moves along his quivering cock until the exquisite taste of him coats my entire tongue. And it's still not enough. Tongue and lips on Coal's shaft, my hand tightens around his sack hard enough that the male's whole body spasms. The magic inside me tightens, the climax that could rip down the stable just one suckle of Coal's cock away.

Stars.

I nip him and pull away sharply, the sudden loss of his cock painful in itself.

A roar escapes Coal's mouth, his body jerking against the restraints, his breaths coming in pants of need that echo my own. His eyes are glazed, purple flecks peppering the brilliant blue. Fighting. Battling. Despite the chill, sweat beads along Coal's brow, fear and desire overwhelming his senses. Bringing him to the brink of sensation.

"Who am I?" I demand, my body screaming to reclaim the connection.

"A mortal," Coal says between clenched teeth. "One who will pay for this."

I show him my teeth, nipping the air the way I just did his cock. "One day, no doubt."

"No. *Now.*" The post holding Coal buckles, the ropes around his wrists snapping like so much twine. Stripes of blood encircle his forearms where the rope cut into his skin.

I stumble back, but there is no escape. Grabbing my hips, Coal lifts me into the air as if I weigh nothing at all.

"I find I'm over the fear of taking you," Coal rasps into my ear. "We'll address *your* demons another time." His breath is hot on the back of my neck as he shoves me over a saddle stand. Padded leather pushes into my stomach, the saddle's horn and high back bracketing me on the right and left. The scent of leather fills my nose.

I writhe, trying to reclaim my feet, but there is no purchase. Not with me bent over, my backside high in the air and neither hands nor feet reaching the floor. Coal presses a hand into the small of my back, his other yanking my trousers down in a single motion. Cold air brushes my exposed flesh, my sex so wet that I feel moisture slithering down my thighs, before Coal sheathes himself inside me so fast and hard that I scream with the pure force of it.

20

LERA

"You smell like you had a good evening yesterday," Autumn says, stepping from thin air into the middle of my bedchamber.

I yelp, dropping the washbasin onto the floor, the liquid soaking my flowing green dress. Fortunately for my soaked clothing, a servant toed into the room while I was sleeping and stoked the fire, leaving the chamber toasty despite the approaching winter. Of course, that also means someone was in the room while my connection with Coal visited my dreams, and if Autumn can smell the arousal even now . . . My face blazes.

"Isn't there something to keep *this* from happening?" I ask, waving my hand in the female's general direction.

Autumn cringes. "Well, there is common decency. You know, that same barrier that stops beings from striding through doors and windows without an invitation. Sorry, Lera. I lost track of where I was." With a sigh, Autumn hoists herself onto the edge of my bed, her usually lively gray eyes drooping with heavy bags.

Stepping around the puddle on the floor, I pull myself up beside Autumn, my feet dangling down from the tall mattress. "What's wrong?"

Autumn pulls up her knees, wrapping her slender arms around them until she looks like a pointy-eared ball wrapped in coral silk. "What's wrong is that I've studied wards for over four centuries." She lays her cheek atop one kneecap. "I had sound-warded the throne room by the time River was just learning to pull a bow. I've built more stable folds and passages through the Gloom than any being in Slait. And I help the Elders Council itself adjust the Citadel's ancient wards. You know what I've *not* studied during the past four hundred years? Ways to go about opening a bloody portal from Lunos to Mors. Because what insane idiot would ever think to do such a thing?"

"And you've been trying to catch up on four hundred years of delinquency in two weeks?" I tug one of Autumn's many blond braids.

She sighs. "Talk to me about something else. River—no, not River. I don't want to know the details of anything River. Coal." Autumn's eyes perk up, her face lifting slightly. "He's pounding a training dummy into its tenth death of the morning, by the way. That's after welcoming the dawn with a freezing dip in the lake. What exactly happened last night?"

I clear my throat. "We had . . . an intellectual discussion on safety while coupling. The first in what I think will be a series of studies."

Autumn blinks once then throws back her head with a melodic roar of laughter. "No wonder the poor bastard can't stop moving. I don't think their cocks can actually explode, but I'd wager my best talisman that he feels like it might."

I smack her with a pillow. "How do you know what Coal's been up to anyway?"

"Kora." Autumn makes a face. "The nosy, overprotective, controlling warrior princess that she is. I swear she combs the bloody grounds every hour. Not even the library is safe."

I open my mouth, then shut it, my eyes narrowing. "Did you step through the Gloom into my bedchamber to avoid her?"

A tiny glint sparkles in Autumn's gray eyes. "Maybe." She cuts her gaze toward me. "Kora might or might not believe I spend too much time thinking and not enough time resting. And she might or might not have some nasty ideas for how to —what does she call it? Ah, yes—give me a break from myself." Autumn bites her lip, her face shifting from outrage to something softer, more vulnerable than I've seen on her. "I've had lovers before, you know," she says quietly. "Male, female, long stints, quick flights of fun, everything. But Kora . . . She sees through to what my soul needs, whether or not my mind even knows it. It's infuriating and intoxicating and . . . Stars, it's so intense I don't know what to do with myself. How do you do it, Lera? Keep being you with *four* overprotective males at your side?"

I consider the question, the answer rising to my lips before I fully know what it will be. "I love them." The words settle through me. "And every time I'm with them, I discover there is more to each one than I thought. As for being me, I'm not the same version of me that those four rescued from Zake's barn. I'm something new, something that's so intertwined with River, Coal, Shade, and Tye that I can't imagine separating. I know that's not much of an answer."

Autumn twines one of her braids around her finger. "It is. It's just a more complicated one than I wanted to hear." A grin flashes across her face. "Maybe I better try doing to Kora whatever you did to Coal last night. I've never seen the male so exquisitely confused as this morning. Speaking of your four"— her voice drops—"what's *that* like? I mean, is it always one or . . .?"

"Yes. Well, kind of." My face blazes as I remember that one night with Tye and Shade on this very bed. I hop off it immediately, restoring the dropped washbasin to its home atop the dresser, my thighs clenching in spite of myself. "I don't even know how anything else would work . . . I mean . . . Never mind. Yes. The answer is yes. One at a time."

Autumn raises a brow.

I grab a towel to soak up the water still on the floor. No. No. *No.* "So what exactly are you conjuring up in that library of yours?" I ask in a pathetic attempt to change the topic.

"Static shields." Autumn's usually musical voice suddenly holds a steel edge. A reminder of the power flaming inside that impish body and brilliant mind. "Something like what Viper tried at your trial, but a great deal more refined." She grins without humor, showing sharp canines. "Once my bastard of a sire shows up, he won't be leaving again without my say so."

Once he shows up. "How long, do you think, until that happens?" I ask. "I feel a bit like we are all bait inside a faulty mousetrap."

"We aren't bait. We are challengers." Autumn's somber tone matches mine at once. "As for how long—not long now, I imagine." Walking to the window, she points to the tallest of the golden-domed towers, where a new flag—this one maroon with a lion of gold—whips in the wind. "If the weeks-long trek to get here wasn't enough of a message, River ran up the king's standard this morning. A claim that Slait Court's rightful ruler is currently in residence."

"So, unless Griorgi wants all of Slait to know he's being challenged, he needs to return at once and be quiet about it, make people think *he's* the ruler in residence." I shake my head. "If this works, it will be the most silent dethroning in history."

"It has to work." Autumn's face darkens. "But either way, we'll find out shortly."

21

RIVER

*B*itter cold bit River's face as he leaned against a great oak in the palace gardens, watching the king's standard flutter in the wind. He'd expected his father to appear within a day of sending up the challenge.

That was over a week ago.

Eight days of checking and rechecking wards, sending out fresh patrols, going over the plan and then going over it again. Eight days of constant vigilance. Vigilance laced with boredom. Coal had broken every post in the training yard. Shade had spent more time in his wolf form than fae, if only to fend off the anxiety.

And now the Slait subjects were starting to ask questions; demand audiences with Griorgi, who they believed was truly in residence; bring by goods the king favored. Even the well-trained palace staff, who knew better than to discuss what was —or was not—truly happening in the palace, were starting to whisper. Yes, on occasion King Griorgi had sequestered himself in his chambers for days—but a week? How could River explain that?

Rumors of an illness would work in the short term, but they were dangerous. Still, better to have servants whispering of a cough than the truth—that Griorgi wasn't there at all. That the prince of Slait had challenged his father's rule and the whole kingdom stood at the edge of turmoil.

The serene gardens were an almost eerie contrast to the tension permeating the air, with their gently rolling lawns, neat stonewalls, and trickling fountains. Weeping willows and broad oaks presided over intimate nooks with moss-covered benches. Vibrant red and orange leaves covered the ground, awaiting the groundskeeper's rake.

River fingered the sword he wore at all times now, as well as the tiny crossbow hanging beneath his coat, a poisoned dart already locked into place. He hoped he didn't shoot his own foot with the damn thing, but it seemed the lesser of the risks.

"I've always considered wars difficult enough on a killing ground," Coal said, leaning beside River on the tree trunk. "Fighting one while pretending no war is happening adds a bit of a new dimension."

River ran a hand through his hair, then stopped, remembering that Leralynn called it a tell of his. "I little want all of Slait taking up arms and killing each other in the name of whatever side of the throne they support. That's the one bloody thing Griorgi and I probably agree on. Where is Leralynn?"

"Attempting to evict Shade from her bedchamber so she can bathe. Last I saw, she was threatening to dump a pitcher of ice water on the bastard's fur."

River nodded, forcing himself to keep his thoughts private. Striking the balance between keeping Leralynn safe and keeping her prisoner was proving . . . difficult. The last time River tried suggesting that she remain with a male at all times, the girl actually removed a set of castration shears from a satchel and silently laid the instrument on the table between them.

Kora was not having any easier time keeping tabs on Autumn. That was the other problem with this weeklong wait —no one could stay at the height of vigilance all the time. Restrictions and precautions that had been followed to the letter on day one were now stretched to accommodate the needs of life.

"River," Coal said.

"I know. I'm *trying* to balance her safety and needs, but—"

"Quiet."

Coal's suddenly hard voice gripped River's chest. Straightening, he followed the direction of the warrior's gaze to a shiny gold pennant that now flew beside the king's standard. *King open to receive petitioners.*

"Get the others, but stay clear of the throne room," River said, already striding to the palace. "We don't want to spook him."

DESPITE THE LONG, anxious wait for this moment, a cold hand still gripped River's throat as he strode into the throne room to find King Griorgi sprawled on the great chair. The long hall was empty but for the male. Between them, the white marble floor where petitioners usually waited gleamed in the sunlight streaming through two-story-tall arched windows. Vases of fresh flowers formed a corridor toward the dais, the bright petals filling the space with perfume. Usually, the smell would help balance the scents of dozens of bodies. Today it simply fed the tension.

Seeing River enter, Griorgi sat up, steepling his hands beneath his chin. As tall as River himself, with broader shoulders, hawkish features, and cold gray eyes, the king was dressed in finely cut blue wool and brown leather. With golden trim and tiny ruby buttons, coupled with an intricate vambrace encircling one muscular forearm, Griorgi looked every inch the ruler he was. Besides the jewelry, the only other change to the male's appearance was a fresh scar carving a jagged line down one cheek all the way to the edge of his right nostril. Leralynn's handiwork. River felt an odd twinge of pride—before remembering where he was.

Years of training made him relax his shoulders and stride toward the dais with the casual confidence expected of a prince. Getting close to the king was vital for the plan to work, making the throne room a better location than River had dared hope for.

"Welcome home, Father," he said, stopping at the dais's edge, just paces from the throne. "I trust both you and your new ally escaped none too scathed from Karnish?"

Griorgi's eyes flashed, his gaze cutting from River to the floor.

Face schooled to stone, River went down on one knee, fist touching his left breast.

Beneath his thick velvet coat, the tiny crossbow was easy to feel, and the small bump made River's heart pound against his ribs. He had to do it now. Get the weapon and fire, leaving no time for discussion, no chance for a magical duel that would bring the palace down around their ears. Anything but a clean shot and people would die. Servants. Innocents. River couldn't allow that. But the male on the throne—he was a rabid dog who needed to be put down before his disease killed more than it already had.

With a tiny motion, River pulled free the knot holding the weapon in place and felt it start to slip down his coat, one inch, two inches—before getting stuck, stars take him.

"That little outburst in Karnish destroyed a good deal of the town, you know," Griorgi said, shaking his head mournfully and gesturing for River to rise. "Warriors buried alive. Limbs crushed. Blood running down the streets." He lowered his voice. "Between you and me, the qoru who weren't adding themselves to the body count were quite pleased—for a short time though. They have little use for corpses."

"And the emperor?" River said, shifting slightly to dislodge the crossbow. The smooth metal handle dropped like ice against his wrist, and River's heart stuttered as he pressed the small weapon into his hip, holding and hiding it with nothing but friction. With painfully tiny motions, he shimmied the crossbow toward his pocket, the image of the thing dropping onto the floor or catching a bit of light making his mouth dry. "Did he find the feast to his satisfaction?"

"The coward stepped into the Subgloom the moment things got ugly. Have you been there, River?" Griorgi shuddered. "If you think the Gloom is dark, the next level down is worse. You feel as if you are beneath water in the dead of night, fighting black liquid each time you move. It's a miracle one can breathe in the Subgloom at all, though the qoru have little trouble. Different anatomy. It was a one-way trip for Jawrar, unfortunately—he can't come up from the Subgloom in Lunos, so back to Mors it was."

A thread of relief ran through River despite his racing pulse—at least Jawrar was no longer in Lunos, just as Autumn had predicted. If Griorgi was telling the truth about the emperor's departure.

River's heart tightened with another thousand questions he wanted to ask now that the crossbow sat inside his pocket, the poisonous dart aimed at Griorgi's chest. He'd thought it would be easy to pull the trigger, had dreamt of doing so countless times since his mother's murder. But now that the moment was here . . . to snuff out his own father's life. He swallowed. Steeled himself.

"Why work with Jawrar?" River asked. "Why not—" He squeezed the trigger.

22

RIVER

*T*he small dart ripped cleanly through the cloth of River's trousers, speeding straight at Griorgi. River hadn't gotten fancy, had fired in the middle of his own question, when the bastard would be least expecting the assault. And he'd aimed for the king's center mass. This was not time for a show. It little mattered where the dart hit—the poison would spread quickly enough.

His body tensed, waiting for the soft slither of needle into flesh. The hiss of surprise.

Clink.

A melodic ring along the floor froze River's blood. *There should be no ringing*, his mind insisted numbly. A *swoosh* perhaps. Maybe a grunt of pain. Or a cry of shock. Not the ringing of metal on marble. River was three paces away. Griorgi could never have gotten a shield up, not at this small distance with no hint of warning. It was impossible.

And yet . . . yet there was the dart, rolling innocuously across the marble floor.

Silence as thick as the Gloom settled over the throne room, until a deep, booming laugh shattered it into a million shards.

"Oh, River, you truly are still a colt." Griorgi adjusted his vine-like vambrace, the deeply inlaid rubies now glistening with mercurial blood. "Mors magic. A present from Jawrar." Griorgi waved his hand in dismissal of River's confusion. "This pretty piece of bloodwork is an armor of sorts, reacting without need for direction from the wearer to shield against physical assault. Takes a bit of practice to use, but quite worth the investment. The qoru find it useful when herding their livestock. The bucks, especially, can be unpredictable."

River's mouth was dry, his heart beating so fiercely against his ribs that it was a wonder the bone didn't crack. "A useful trinket," he said, his mind racing for the next step and conjuring nothing better than stalling. Autumn's static shield ward was working well, as of yesterday, and she would likely bring the amulet with the inscribed rune once she heard Coal's summons. River pointed toward the vambrace with his chin. "Where might I get one?"

Griorgi laughed again. "I'd get you one at the next opportunity, though the cost of keeping it charged might turn your stomach. Not everyone who likes meat can slaughter the animals, and you are much too dainty for such things."

"I might be persuaded to change my mind," River said, releasing a small breath as one of the side doors opened to reveal Coal, Tye, and Shade—the latter bloody and swaying on his feet. River pushed his worries aside for later. If the males were here, it meant Autumn likely had her shield in place, ready to keep Griorgi from getting away no matter what happened.

"I'm glad you see it that way." Ignoring Coal and the others, the king pulled a set of bracelets from the inside of his tunic. The design somewhat echoed the vambrace he wore, though the metal was dull and, in place of rubies, held a line of stones so dark they swallowed the light.

Just like that shield Emperor Jawrar had erected to protect against River's attack.

"Put these on." Griorgi tossed the cuffs to River, who caught them on instinct.

At once, bile rose into his throat, the corruption and wrongness of the things twisting his magic.

Griorgi held up a hand, his eyes suddenly as dark as the obsidian stones. "There is something I'd like you to see, River —before you do something unwise. Wait here." Rising from his throne, Griorgi stepped into the Gloom, the air about him rippling as he disappeared. Two heartbeats later, the male was back.

And he had Leralynn with him.

River froze.

From the girl's wet hair and robe, he guessed Griorgi had snatched her right as she was finishing a bath. Writhing against Griorgi's grip on the back of her neck, Leralynn curled in on herself, her right eye swollen shut, the left hooded with deep bruising. A gag in her mouth prevented speech—but didn't mask the sounds of fury and horror in her throat.

Terror filled River, each muscle in his body tightening with the need to fight. To kill. He didn't notice rising or filling himself with all his magic until he had already done it. Knew his quint brothers were doing the same on the edge of the room. One more breath and River would bring down the whole damn palace. Half the kingdom. Anything.

"Stop." Griorgi shoved Leralynn to her knees, exposing the girl's neck—a collar of darkness encircled her throat. A leash running from the collar was looped around Griorgi's wrist.

"Coal can explain the details of this little tool to you, I'm sure, but in short—"

Leralynn jerked, her hands clawing at her throat.

"Won't help, luv," Griorgi told the girl, his voice filled with perverted sympathy. "Only River's obedience can help you now, I'm afraid." He gestured at the bracelets in River's grip.

Leralynn shook her head, her one good eye flashing in defiance. *No. Don't.*

Nausea rolled through River, his pounding heart stilling as Leralynn's lips darkened from a healthy pink to a deadly, airless blue. Another moment and the bastard would kill her by accident.

"Stop." River held up the bracelets. Whatever the corrupt things did, they would do it to him, not Leralynn. That itself was better. "Let her go and I'll do as you say."

"Get to it, then." Griorgi waved his hand. At the other end of the leash, Leralynn drew a rasping breath, as if granted a tiny sliver of air. "I'm attempting to let her live so as to keep you from throwing a tantrum in the middle of Slait and killing hundreds of my people. But putter about too much longer and I will snap this pretty little pet's neck and find another incentive."

Leralynn's face darkened again, all sounds of breath stopping.

River could feel Coal, Tye, and Shade's rage and panic from across the room, pulsing off them in waves. They wanted to do something—something dangerous, possibly fatal for one or all of them—and they would. If River didn't do something first.

His throat closed, his hands obeying. There was no choice, not if Leralynn was to live. All his plans, his shields, his ideas— how quickly none of them mattered any longer. Eyes on the girl's neck, River snapped the odd metal around one wrist and then the other, shuddering as a cold rush chilled his core. As if liquid Gloom had spilled into his blood.

On instinct, he reached down for his magic, seeking its comfort to fend off the darkness. The power blazed to life—and struck that dull metal around his wrists. For a moment, an utter absence of sensation raced through his body. And then a shock wave painful enough to drop him to his knees.

"Don't touch your magic," Coal yelled, though it was much too late.

Leralynn gasped, stretching toward River.

"Quiet, pet." Griorgi yanked on the girl's leash so hard that she fell backwards. "It's time for us to be leaving."

As Leralynn's back connected with the floor, a bloodcurdling roar echoed off the stone walls. That roar was the only warning anyone got before a seven-hundred-pound tiger streaked across the room at Griorgi. The large cat's green eyes flashed with wildness, his teeth glistening murder—his mind oblivious to any defenses the king had in place.

23

LERA

I scream into my gag as Tye's tiger rushes for Griorgi. Scrambling to my feet, I throw my hands forward to ward off the animal—as if such a gesture could possibly halt the male before he meets whatever Mors-backed shield Griorgi has around him. Pain shoots across my ribs.

The great cat pivots, changing direction with a predator's practiced grace.

A breath of relief fills my tortured lungs—only to freeze again.

Pushing off the marble floor, Tye's tiger pounces. Seven hundred pounds of muscle shove into *me* so hard that my bones scream. The leash Griorgi has around my neck snaps in two, nearly taking my neck with it. Staggering beneath Tye's force, I crash into the nearest wall, the room blinking in and out of darkness. When my eyes clear enough to focus, I find the tiger crouching over me, his maw flashing all his flesh-tearing teeth.

No fear. No fear. No fear. I force myself to inhale slowly despite my racing heart.

"Lera!" Shade shouts.

Tye's tiger whirls on him. The low, menacing rumble coming from the cat's chest carries nothing of his fae partner's reason. Twisting his great head around the room, the tiger roars the same warning to all the males in it. *Mine. Stay away.*

"Stay back, Shade," I call, careful not to look at the dark-haired male. To do nothing to give Tye's tiger reason to worry for his territory. My mind races. With River shackled, we are all at Griorgi's mercy.

"Well, this is intriguing, isn't it?" Griorgi straightens his blue jacket cuffs, watching the scene unfold with an arched brow. His corrupted resemblance to my River fills me with sick dread, his dark bulk and sour scent as disturbing now as when he snatched me up from the bathtub, leering at the naked parts of me meant only for my males. The rising scream he clamped inside me with one hard hand feels like it's still there, tearing at my throat. As are the lupine whimpers I heard through the door when the bastard stepped out, leaving me bound. Griorgi examines his fingernails for a moment. "One mindless beast, one mortal whore, a princeling with a bit in his mouth, and two sets of damaged goods. Quite an army. Tell the brains of your operation to stop braiding her hair and get out here."

"Autumn isn't he—" River's protest dissolves into a bellow of pain. I flinch. The normally smooth planes of his beautiful face are contorted, his large hands pulling at the bracelets with such force that I fear he'll break his bones.

I realize I'm moving only when Tye's tiger roars his displeasure, forcing me back to the ground. River's howl of pain continues on and on until he slumps unconscious to the floor. I hold back a scream. Blood drips from his wrists and mouth, a puddle of viscous red slithering across the white marble floor.

Griorgi sighs. "Well, one can't have everything he desires all at once." He crooks a finger, beckoning Coal and Shade to him. "I will take only those with a full set of wits, small as they might be." He points to River. "Pick that up and let's move. You know what will happen to your commander if you even consider disobeying."

Terror races through my veins as Coal and Shade hold the slumping River between them, Griorgi herding the trio into the Gloom. As Coal steps into the rippling air, he turns toward me long enough to mouth, "Stay away, mortal."

"WE HAVE TO GO AFTER THEM." My mouth is thick, my swollen face moving sluggishly, as one of Kora's quint sisters helps me out of the throne room. With Tye's tiger on alert, it took the female an hour just to get to me without being eaten, and twice as long as that to help me into the corridor. I may not have my own magic or be able to sense the bond as acutely as they can, but I can *feel* my males growing farther away from me with every minute that passes. Dull panic spreads through me with each heartbeat. They're gone. I can't believe they're gone. I grab the woman's clothes, clutching the material in my stiff fingers. Image after image of horror races through my thoughts. "Where is Autumn?"

"In her bedchamber. Shouting loudly enough to wake the stars." Putting a hand around my waist, the female guides me to Autumn's room. I barely register the richly upholstered walls or gilded sconces, the thick carpet that swallows our footsteps. When she opens the door to unleash Autumn's shrieking, I realize the place is warded for sound.

"There was no choice," Kora shouts over Autumn's cries. "He'd just have snatched you as well." Sitting on Autumn's bed, Kora holds my flailing friend in a bear hug, the gouges along Kora's skin betraying signs of a battle. Seeing me enter, Kora turns Autumn to face me. "Look." She shakes Autumn's shoulders. "Griorgi would have killed her. There was no choice. There isn't one now."

Autumn gulps a breath, her puffy eyes widening when she sees my bruised face. "We have to go after them."

"You can't go after them," Kora snaps, plainly not for the first time. Her blue eyes flash at me. "We go after him now, and the bastard gets everything he wants. You. Lera. The males. Everything. We *will* win the war, but we lost this battle the moment those shackles snapped onto River's wrists."

"I—" Autumn and I both say together.

"No!" Kora glares at us both, her tone chilling the room. "There will be no suicide. If either of you thinks you will face Griorgi and survive just now, you can start by trying to get past me. And then that rabid tiger in the throne room. I'll have the servants ready to mop up whatever bloody bits are left behind."

24

LERA

"Tye?" The throne room door shuts behind me on silent hinges, the midnight bell's distant toll a surreal sound against the darkness. Lifting the lantern, I survey the cold space.

Across the marble floor, the tiger cracks open one green eye and watches me curiously.

"You have no idea what happened, do you?" I bite my lip, wondering if I might not envy the animal's oblivion. On the off chance that the other males are somewhere close, I reach out with my mind, trying to feel for a hint of Coal's essence. I come up with nothing. Again. Only an emptiness that coats my core in darkness.

For the first time, I fully understand Shade's choice to remain in wolf form after his twin's death. I'd give a great deal to dull my emotions just now. *They are alive,* I remind myself. *You'd feel their deaths if they happened.*

Yes, River, Shade, and Coal are alive. Whether they're

wishing it were otherwise just now is a different question entirely.

Wincing, I set down the pair of blankets and bowl of milk I brought along. Despite the hours that the palace healer spent working on me, my body still hurts every time I move, but the pain is welcome. Deserved. I might be unable to disagree with Kora's reasoning that we need a plan before taking action, but that does nothing for the hole in my chest. I spread out one of the blankets. "We can't let you out of here in tiger form, but I thought lying on a marble floor might be . . . I brought this."

Just when I think the tiger will not condescend to move, the great cat lumbers to his feet and pads over. Lowering his face into the bowl, he sneezes, sending droplets of milk flying. Lifting a pink nose, the tiger glares at me disapprovingly.

I cross my arms. "I'm aware that you aren't a vegetarian, but if you think I'm hauling a plateful of dead rodents in here for your dinner, you have another thing coming."

Tye's tiger shifts his whiskers, his expressive green eyes saying, "*Who said they needed to be dead?*"

Ignoring the indignant feline, I take the second blanket into a corner as far from the throne—from the memory of Griorgi—as possible and curl into a ball. Tye might be a tiger just now, but I'll share a marble floor with him over a bed alone any day. Or night.

I WAKE to the scent of clean lavender sheets mixed with a pine-and-citrus smell that wraps around me as tightly as the down coverlet. Blinking against the morning sunlight, I find Tye in his fae form, sprawled on the bed beside me, green eyes trained on my face. His heavy arm is a solid weight on my waist.

"Where—how—what time is it?" My words muddle in my mouth. It hurts to move. It hurts to live.

Tye brushes a hand down my hair. "About ten in the morning. Long enough for Autumn to have filled me in on what happened." His face is tight, the pain behind his eyes as palpable as my own. "I shifted back around dawn and thought relocating off a marble floor was worth the effort."

Reaching out, Tye pulls me against him, burying my face in his muscular shoulder while his arms encircle me tightly. The *lub-dub, lub-dub* of his heart echoes through my flesh, spurring on my own.

"It isn't fair," I whisper, lifting my head enough to find his green eyes. My hands tighten on Tye's bare skin, nails digging into his flesh. "The two of us here, in this soft down bed, while the others are held in shackles."

The corners of the male's mouth tighten but he doesn't pull away, his own hands digging hard into my muscles instead. "No. It isn't."

I stare down at him. The hard lines of his face, his penetrating gaze, the sheer power vibrating off his sculpted muscles—he's a citadel of strength. The rage of a battle I never got to fight in the throne room surges through me, making my heart pound. A fire blazes to life in my chest, wanting to burn the world out of sheer spite. To do something, anything, to punch through the veil of despair. I draw a sharp breath. And, with the next bang of my heart, close my mouth over Tye's.

My tongue punches into his mouth, assaulting his with savage fury.

Tye growls, the sound vibrating his chest. Mouth still on

mine, he twists us to shove my shoulders into the mattress, which bounces slightly beneath the sudden attack. Tye's teeth scrape my lip as he pulls away, towering over my body as he straddles my hips. His hard hands grab my shirt, ripping it in a single, deafening motion.

The tearing fabric bites my skin, my heart quickening in response. My muscles coil, buck, fight against the immovable weight pinning me to the bed. "It isn't fair," I half shout, half sob, the pounding of memories bruising my soul. Griorgi's leering shadow. His hand over my mouth. Bathwater splashing everywhere. River twisting in pain on the throne-room floor. Coal's blue eyes blazing into mine one more time before disappearing into the Gloom. "It isn't—"

Tye catches my wrist, and I realize I've just struck him. Was going for another blow. Overpowering me, the male pins my assaulting arms over my head in a vicelike grip. With his thighs bracketing my hips, one hand pressing my wrists into the mattress, he grips my gaze.

I let loose a shuddering breath, my sex clenching as helplessly as the rest of me.

Tye's nostrils flare, no doubt taking in the harsh arousal. As if my body, unable to fight, demands a substitution.

Baring himself with an efficient motion, his green eyes fierce over mine, Tye positions his shaft at my opening and thrusts hard. Again. Again. The throbbing head of his cock finds the vulnerable spot inside me and gives no mercy, each stroke igniting a mix of pleasure and pain. A carnal hurt so strong that it echoes through my body, fighting back the darkness, if only for a moment.

"Harder," I say through clenched teeth, riding the furiously growing need inside until it explodes beyond control. My body teeters on the edge of release, flashes of memory interspersing with blasts of sensation. I jerk against the restraints, flailing for freedom that I don't know what I'd do with.

Tye's hand on my wrists tightens. Holding me in place with his weight, his legs, his gaze, the male grants me no freedom, no quarter, no choice but to feel *him* to the exclusion of the world. His chiseled chest and shoulders rise over me, damp with sweat, filling my view. The rhythmic, relentless pounding through my wetness grows to consume my universe. When I open my mouth, Tye's lips descend punishingly over mine. Taking away even my speech.

Surrender washes over me with his next stroke, my mind quieting to let zings of pleasure shoot through my sex, down the backs of my legs. My toes curl, my fingers tightening against air as my channel clenches around the male's hardness. When the tsunami of release comes, tears finally flow with it.

Tye cradles me against him when we finish, letting go only long enough to dip a washcloth into water. Wiping the moist towel over my face, he gently traces the slopes of my cheekbones, my bruises that are a pale yellow now, thanks to time and healing magic. The water's coolness is welcome against my steaming skin, as is the slow, rhythmic brush of Tye's breath against my hair.

"Tell me we'll get them back," I say into his chest.

"We'll get them back," answers a voice too high to be Tye's.

Shifting, I turn my face toward the door and find Autumn, fully dressed in determination.

LERA

"I combed the throne room this morning," Autumn says, pacing back and forth along the oak table in one of the palace library's alcoves. Around us, shelves of books reach up to a vaulted ceiling, hanging candelabras bathing the space in warm light. Seated at the book-laden table, Kora, Tye, and I inhale the scent of aged paper and bindings as we follow Autumn's progress with our eyes. Without River's firm opinions, Coal's guarding presence around the edges, and Shade's comforting warmth, our group feels thin, wobbly. We all try to ignore it.

Autumn quickens her steps. Turns. Walks back, fingers fiddling with the tips of her silver braids. I don't know what fills me with more dread—her ragged, unpolished nails or her simple, mindless outfit. Black tights and a man's sweater that looks like it may be on backwards. When I realize by its scent that it must be River's, my heart lodges in my throat. Missing a brother can hardly be easier than missing a quint mate. "I found several folds in the Gloom, but only one that's new.

Following *that* direction, and knowing Griorgi's prior choices, and his intended goal of—"

"Just say it, Autumn." I rest my elbows on the table, my heart pounding. "Do you know where they are?"

She swallows, her gaze skimming over Tye's. "I know where they are going to be in ten days' time."

"The Blaze capital." Tye's jaw tightens with understanding. "In a week and a half, Blaze will be celebrating Samhain—as if spirits and darkness warrant a bloody festival. Bonfires, masquerades, trials of fear and courage—the lore is that by showing the darkness how close you can get to it and not be afraid, you'll intimidate it into staying put for another year." He rubs his face. "Point is, everyone will be out in hordes, celebrating and drinking. A perfect target."

"Won't it be the same in all the courts though?" I ask.

Autumn shakes her head. "Blaze is the only court to celebrate Samhain. Many in Blaze have a fire-magic affinity, like Tye, so I think they are partial to the tradition."

"Stars," Tye says. "Around that time, no one might even notice a bloody portal from Mors opening until Griorgi has slaughtered half the capital."

Autumn nods, her face grim as she turns an open book toward us. "It isn't just that Blaze will be distracted. Samhain actually is the time when the wards between Lunos and Mors are weakest, especially where Blaze is. Between the celebration, the weakened wards, and River's blood, Griorgi has everything he needs for a major offensive."

"If the bastard catches Blaze unawares, they will not stand a chance." I slide my hand into Tye's, squeezing his callused fingers. "So we go warn Blaze. With only the two of us, we should be able to beat Griorgi there."

Autumn stops pacing, her gray eyes flashing in our direction. "Three of us."

"Eight of us," Kora drawls, lifting her chin as if daring anyone to contradict her.

Tye shakes his head. "You can't go, Sparkle."

"Tye is right." I wince. "You are the only Slait royal left, and someone has to keep the court thriving no matter what happens. Plus, you'll need to coordinate with the Citadel, see if they can help somehow."

Autumn opens her mouth to protest, only to shut it when Tye sends tiny sparks of fire dancing like shackles around her wrists.

"There is also the bit about you sharing Griorgi's blood," he says softly, his green eyes apologetic. "You said ancient magics are fueled by blood and that there isn't a bloodline in Slait stronger than Griorgi's. If things go poorly, we can't let him use you too."

TYE AND I leave as soon as we can manage, which is before dawn the following morning—Autumn having stayed up all night to work out a carefully sketched map of exactly which Gloom passages to use and when. Apparently, between the Gloom's shifting nature and its life-energy-sapping existence, planning a balanced and expedient route takes a good deal of calculation. All the formulas make one thing clear: Tye and I will need nearly every one of those ten days to get to Blaze on time.

"How is it even possible to draw a map for something that keeps shifting?" I ask, yawning over my coffee as Autumn drums her fingers on the parchment she is sending us off with.

Kora gives me a dark look.

Autumn blinks, rubbing her eyes. "The same way seafarers use charts. Last I checked, the ocean's currents and winds seldom stay still either."

"Thank you, Sparkle," Tye says with a seriousness that twists my stomach into a knot. A knot that only gets heavier when the pair of us move out, racing against time.

OUR FIRST SEVEN days pass in a quiet blur, each of us lost in our own thoughts and worries, the only comfort coming with sleep, wrapped tightly in each other's arms. Or, when too cold, the tiger's fur. I find myself pressing my car to Tye's heartbeat each night, letting it stand in for each of my males, willing them to stay alive until we can reach them.

The landscape morphs more with each day we travel, the land's magic affecting the soil and vegetation in the Light and Gloom both. In place of the neutral lands' dizzying peaks and Slait's lush forests, Blaze stretches into wide savannahs, with trees far enough apart to keep the canopy from closing. On the ground, the brittle grass rises in shades of yellow and brown, often with patches of orange-tinged soil showing through the strands. The sun's power grows, slowing me down as we move deeper into the heart of Blaze, reminding me of the trial arena. Only the bright-blue moss growing in the Gloom remains a constant.

"How long have you been away from Blaze?" I ask Tye as we slide back into the Gloom on the morning of our eighth day. The drab colors and sounds chill my core as always.

"Not counting the recent excursion to Karnish?" Tye turns to look over his shoulder at me, his dapple stallion bristling unhappily as grass crunches underfoot with a dull crackle. "About three hundred years, since I joined the quint. No, wait, I think I was arrested in Slait before that. So, a long time."

A tinge of sadness spiders over my skin. "And you've not talked to your family since?"

"No." Drawing the sword strapped across his back, Tye hacks a thick clump of moss off a low-hanging branch. "Damn parasite. I swear it's spreading more each time we step here."

"This?" Reaching out to another patch of moss, I brush my fingers through the bright, almost glowing, strands. They feel as thick as a tiger's fur, warm and velvety.

Tye cringes. "Don't touch it."

"Why not? It's pretty. The only thing with any color here."

"Pretty?" Tye snorts. "You know *why* it's colorful and bright?" Tye plucks off a piece, hissing as he holds the blue tuft on his bare palm for a few seconds. When he finally drops it, the skin blisters with red burns. "The moss feeds off magic. The only native to the Gloom, and it preys on everyone who enters." Reclaiming his sword, Tye hacks off another blue clump, this one as big as a sunflower. "Coal says the qoru are battling it constantly too. The one and only thing Lunos and Mors have in common."

"Maybe it just doesn't know what to do with me, since I've no magic of my own." I pull my hand away, feeling the loss of the moss's warmth. "Still, it feels like the friendliest thing out here. As if it's keeping us company."

The words hang in the air between us, underscoring the others' absence. I swallow, turning away. A few moments later, Tye rides up close enough to put a strong hand on my knee. "Let's take a few hours in the Light, Lilac Girl," he says with a cheerfulness I know he doesn't feel. "Dead rescuers are not nearly as effective as living ones, and I think the horses could use a bit of fresh air. Plus, I've something better than moss to show you."

The something better turns out to be the horizon of civilization, the distant peak of the Blaze Royal Palace beckoning from far-off plains. Its gilded, spindly towers rise into the air like twisting flames, catching the sunlight. "It looks like we are almost there." I stretch my lower back. "Ahead of schedule."

Tye snorts. "We are neither. It's all much farther than it looks."

Despite my inclination to not believe him, the male turns out to be right. With little by way of reference, moving through the savannah and a slowly growing density of small villages—clusters of low earthen huts and wide-eyed fae children—feels like a great deal of forward motion without much to show for it. By the time we finally enter the populated area at the outskirts of Blaze's capital city, Ferno, it's early evening.

Only two days until Samhain remain and decorations adorn almost every door and fence. Every post and window is strung with garlands and lights, and many walls show off chalked sketches of animal skeletons, tormented spirits, and nose-less, sharp-toothed . . . "Are those qoru?" I point to one of the better drawings, this one covering the wall of a busy pub. Here, bright lines of chalk depict a pair of qoru sitting cross-legged at a small, round table, each creature nursing a mug of bubbling brew.

"Aye." Tye's usually amused voice is tight, as if braced for a blow. "My people take Samhain to its proper absurdity. When the fires are lit the night after next, the whole city will look like a flaming river—with enough colts standing so close to the flames to prove their courage that the healers will be busy for the next month."

I give Tye a sidelong glance, wondering whether he realizes how closely Blaze's Samhain spirit fits with his own flex mastery. "Ferno is a great deal busier than Slait, isn't it?" I say instead, taking in the chaotic streets. The place feels more like a huge, overcrowded village from the mortal lands than Slait's stately capital. The closely packed sandstone and orange-clay buildings seem to tumble over each other like a natural organism, reaching multiple stories into the air so they almost lean over our narrow stone street. Fae bustle in every direction, some overhead on walkways that crisscross the road, some brushing right past us on feet and horseback—all so busy with their own errands that at first we seem to be anonymous. A feeling that lasts all of about one minute. As we ride, a turned head or two morphs into hushed whispers, which soon give way to hordes of children running into the street to see the novelties for themselves. All are dressed in loose, billowing fabrics of white and red and orange, long-sleeved tunics and pants that billow in the wind like a tribute to the fire magic Blaze is known for.

"Slait sprawls," Tye says finally, a smile in his voice. "Blaze —Ferno City, especially—is more of an anthill. It's had to grow up and down and over itself instead of out, by virtue of being situated over the only source of abundant groundwater for hundreds of miles in any direction." Tye sighs. "And by the time we are halfway through, with how densely populated it is, the whole damn place is going to know we're here. Are you hungry, lass? We might as well get this over with."

"Get what—" I cut off as a beautiful pointy-featured female piling wood on a future bonfire drops her bundle and gasps, one hand pointed at Tye.

"Tyelor? Stars. You *are* him, aren't you?" Rushing over, she all but knocks into Tye's stallion, who dances disapprovingly. The female wipes her hands on her apron. "*The* Tyelor? Flex champion?"

Swinging down from the saddle, Tye bows hastily. "Aye, lass." His coy smile and sparkling eyes are such a perfect mask that I doubt anyone but me sees the heart-tearing pain beneath. "And an awfully hungry one. Can you point my mate and me to a decent dinner?"

Mate. The word rolls through me with a possessive warmth, even as it brings weighing stares.

"That's a mortal." The female makes a face.

In my dusty black riding tights, billowing white shirt, and black leather vest, I suddenly go from feeling strong to feeling like a bug under this random female's shoes. It's a harsh reminder of what humans are to fae in most of Lunos— nothing. Or worse than nothing.

"She is?" Tye blinks, helping me down from Sprite's back while a boy runs forward with an offer to take the horses. "I'd not noticed."

"Enough gabbing." An older female comes out of what looks like an inn, her wrinkled face spreading into a smile. "Welcome home, Master Tyelor. We've never stopped cheering for you, you know. One of our own colts rising up to challenge the prince himself. Whatever happened at the end, we all tell our youngsters of you. Come, bring your guest in and we'll set you up with some supper."

The tips of Tye's ears darken, but he covers the blush with a bow, straightening just in time to catch a tripping boy who clutches a wooden mug in one hand and a sharp knife in the other.

"Master Tyelor! Master Tyelor!" the boy says, extending

both items to Tye as the male sets him back on his feet. "I'm training in flex too. Would you carve your name for me? My coach says—ow!" He yelps, protesting loudly as the previously simpering female grabs his ear and escorts him away.

"You are more famous than River," I say quietly, following Tye to a table that the innkeeper has ordered to be set. "Was it like this before you left?"

My male nods once and pushes the bread toward me, the aroma of yeast and fresh flour filling the air. Breaking into the thick crust, I study Tye over the haze of false privacy. The whole dining room is watching us. Watching him. The realization seeps through me slowly, mixing with Tye's words and secrets. He wasn't just an athlete; he was a hero. A beacon of hope, showing the low-born commoners that work and dedication *could* take them to their dreams. And if I know Tye, he thinks he let down every one of them.

I slide my hand along the tabletop to grip Tye's fingers, my thumb caressing his callused knuckles. *I'm here,* I tell him silently. *And I love you.*

Tye's gaze penetrates mine, as if anchoring itself in my soul to the exclusion of the world. The feline intensity makes my heart stutter, the sudden need to be closer so overpowering that my breath catches in my throat. My male. This glorious, mischievous, wounded, loyal warrior is mine. History and present and all.

"Well, if it isn't you," a cold voice snaps. The female stalking toward us looks sweaty from a hard ride. Red hair pulled back into a thick braid, she wears the livery of a palace servant and glares at Tye with icy green eyes.

A muscle in Tye's jaw ticks. "Saritta." Rising from his chair, he bows to the newcomer. "An unexpected pleasure, running into you so . . . efficiently."

I rise too, my body tense, an acrid possessiveness washing over me.

The female snorts. "What were you expecting, Tyelor? A parade? A noose? With you, one can never quite tell." Saritta's face swivels toward me, her nose wrinkling in disgust. "And what is that?"

Tye pulls me close against his body, his brown leather armor creaking, his hard muscles a wall of support at my back. "Saritta, allow me to introduce my quint-bonded and mate, Leralynn. Lera, this is Saritta. My sister."

26

LERA

*S*aritta freezes, the gaze she pins me with changing from dismissive to intrusive. Her scent of sweat, soap, and starch lingers in the air between us.

"Mate?" Her nose wrinkles, her perfect features contorting from surprise to confusion back to unfiltered disgust. "You mated with a human? That is low even for you, Tyelor." Putting her hands on the tabletop before her brother, she leans forward, her voice lowering. "If you came back to ask for Mother's blessing, you can go back where you came from, you bastard. You've created enough problems for our family without piling more dung onto the heap."

When Tye's face remains unreadable enough to rival Coal's, Saritta spins on her heels and strides out of the inn.

I am on her heels before I can think, ignoring Tye's protests behind me. My hand closes around the female's wrist just as she steps outside. With the breeze, the smell of harsh soap is even more prominent. That, coupled with the roughness of her skin and strength of her muscles, tells me the female labors hard at the palace. "Your brother returns after several centuries and you intercept him to do what, exactly?" I demand. "Do you even care why we came?"

Saritta looks down at me, pulling her hand from my grasp in a single, hard jerk. "Do you know how much our mother sacrificed for your *mate* to twirl around a horizontal bar? What it cost her to let him play athlete while she worked to the bone to feed us?"

"I—"

"Go ask your mate how he threw decades of her sacrifice away for a night of drink." Centuries of hurt and pain roll through Saritta's green gaze. "How he left our mother and me with nothing but debt—walked away rather than face what he'd done. How he never even acknowledged that we'd been attacked, much less came home to help. After all our mother did for him, Tyelor *left* her the one time she needed him. If you've any brains in that mortal head of yours, you would turn tail and run as bloody far from him as you can."

I stare at Saritta, my mind sifting through and rearranging her words in search of meaning. "You think Tye left you for fear of facing up to a mistake?" I say incredulously. "You actually think that the male with the biggest heart in Lunos ignored an attack on his family because he *didn't* care for you? That after giving up his youth and his tiger for flex, he walked away from it all for a night of fun and debauchery?"

"When the night of debauchery leads to forfeiting the one competition that might have changed our social standing and future? Yes, my brother is enough of a coward to run after that." Saritta's eyes narrow. "And what's this babbling about a tiger?"

"Tye's animal form." I frown, wondering if I'm misusing the words. "The tiger Tye shifts into."

"Tye isn't a shifter." Saritta snorts. "And if he tells you he is, he's lying. Get used to that, girl, if you're with him. Shifter." She shakes her head. "Shifters don't survive flex beyond colts' school games. You stand at a crossroads, lass. Open your eyes to the male sitting across the table from you, or else drink in his lies until, one day, the world tells you the truth."

"You are wrong," I ground out, putting all the weight of my pain behind it, my missing quint mates, my love for Tye, so fierce inside me that it almost hurts. I catch Saritta's green gaze, though the female, nearly as tall as her brother, towers over me. "You have no notion of what Tye is. No notion of why he left. And certainly no notion of what he's done since. And if you care too little to bother finding out, stay the bloody hell out of our way."

I RETURN to the table to find it empty. The innkeeper scurries over to assure me that Tyelor has settled the bill over her protests and ordered the rest of our dinner sent to our room. After imploring me to bring the male back downstairs, where so many of his fans are already filling the dining room, she sends me up with a bottle of wine and the promise of a warm bath to be brought up at once.

Climbing the stairs, I slowly push open the door to a small but clean room. The crackling fire warms the space, sending shadows dancing across the floor. Bare to the waist, Tye stands staring out the window. The light sculpts his muscles with an artist's skill, but when I approach to wrap my arms around him, I find nothing but rock-hard tension beneath his skin.

"Saritta—" I start softly.

"Saritta has a right to her grudges." Tye turns and walks

over to the washbasin, his magic heating the water to a steaming simmer. "And we've not come for a family reunion. I have sent a letter to the palace with River's seal on it. Prince Xane will grant us an audience tomorrow morning. And then it'll be him, not Saritta, who we need to convince of the truth."

27

TYE

*T*ye's fire seeped into the cold marble floor of the throne room in which he and Lera knelt, the small release of magic the only way to keep his fury at bay.

"Let me see if I have this right." Sitting cross-legged on the throne, Prince Xane leaned forward, his forearms on his thighs. "King Griorgi and Prince River of Slait are currently burrowing a passage into Blaze Court in order to join forces with Mors's Emperor Jawrar and take over Lunos?"

The ill-concealed laughter behind Xane's voice escaped, echoing off the tapestry-covered walls of the throne room before dissolving into little gasping giggles. Rising to his feet, he strode down the three steps separating his dais from where Tye and Lera still knelt. The prince was every bit as buffed and polished and ridiculous as Tye remembered, his silky strawberry-blond hair tied back in a low ponytail, topped with a tiny gold crown that mimicked the twisting, flame-like towers of the Blaze Royal Palace. His green eyes were lined with brown kohl to accentuate them, though perhaps he hoped no one noticed. His features were delicate—almost pretty—his muscles smooth and well-mannered. "Truly, Tyelor, you spin the most entertaining tales. Still, it is a pleasure to have you back." The last was said with enough distaste to make Xane's true feeling about Tye clear.

Tye shot Lera a silent warning to keep her mouth shut, though he could feel the lass trembling with indignation. This morning, he had helped her into the one fine dress she brought for this very occasion, a stunningly simple emerald-green silk that brought out the red in her hair and hugged her slim torso with a wide band of black lace, leaving her shoulders and clavicle temptingly bare. He had wished with every breath that Autumn were around for that part—but changed his mind as soon as he realized that helping her into a flowing dress meant getting to run his hands over her skin, to stand close behind her and inhale her heady lilac scent.

And yet it had all been for nothing, it seemed. The day was *not* going well. Despite arriving at the palace over six hours earlier and spelling out the problem in numerous notes, Xane had only now granted them an audience. Once the damn prince realized his error in having wasted precious time, there would be hell to pay—and Tye wanted Lera nowhere near Xane's sights when that happened.

"This is neither jest nor tale, Your Highness." Tye spoke coolly, though his hands tingled to wrap themselves around the bastard's slender neck. For everything. "The king must be informed—"

"I'll worry about the king. Come, let us speak like the old friends we are." Xane extended his hand to Tye, as if the kneeling had been a formality of no consequence. "Have your say and leave."

Rising to his feet, Tye offered a hand to Lera and followed

the prince into a sitting room off the main hall, where deep leather chairs and shelves of books strived and failed to create an intimate atmosphere. If River's library hosted his favorite reads and maps of Lunos, Xane's was a decoration designed solely to impress. Books from top military strategists, histories of flex, designs for weaponry. All as untouched as the day they were purchased. Midafternoon sunlight fell in harsh stripes across the room through narrow defensive windows. No glass, as Blaze's royals—nearly all with fire-magic affinities—could simply light fires in any hearth to keep the room warm.

Tye's gaze fell on Xane's Realm Championship trophy, displayed in a place of honor on a slim marble pedestal, a delicate lantern suspended right overhead—as if the prince had actually earned the title.

"Wine?" Xane asked, pouring a glass for himself from a crystal decanter and hesitating over Tye's. His slim, bejeweled fingers looked like they hadn't touched a horizontal bar in years. Nary a callus or chalk-filled crease in sight. "I apologize . . . After what happened, I hadn't considered that you might be staying away from spirits. I indulge in a bit now and then, though the old training regimen does leave a shadow even still. I swear I hear my trainer's voice each time I so much as smell fermenting grapes."

If by "what happened," you're referring to the attack you ordered on my family so you could have a pretty trophy, then wine would be welcome. Tye bit his tongue. He could either spend the next hour butting heads with Xane about history—a debate that would most likely land him in the dungeon—or put the prince's worries about Tye challenging his victory to rest and return to the matter at hand.

Tye drew a breath, forcing himself to stay calm. Xane controlled access to the king and Blaze Royal Guard. Without the prince's agreement, there was no option. No way of preparing for tomorrow. "Wine would be well taken, Your Highness," Tye said lightly, draining his glass and holding it out for a refill. "It has been a pleasure of mine for some time now. Apparently, some of us never learn reason." Tye could feel the tension creeping into Lera's shoulders at this without even looking at her. Silently, he willed her to keep her cool again. "About tomorrow's Samhain celebration, did you read the letter I brought from Princess Autumn? Does it not confirm my warning?"

"Autumn? The little female with the roundest ass in Slait?" Xane smacked his lips. "While she would be more than welcome to tell me in person all about the scary monsters hiding in the Gloom, the letter just fails to get a proper rise out of me." Xane shakes his head. "Tyelor, you know I'd do anything for you, but if I go to my father with these tales, he will laugh me out of the throne room. The Slait princess is known for her . . . What's the word? Ah, theories. Not even King Griorgi takes the lass seriously."

"The Citadel and Elders Council themselves take her seriously." Tye checked himself. Hard. Leaning forward, he put his elbows on his thighs. He wasn't here as Xane's subject or old flex rival. He was here as one of the Citadel's elite warriors, whether he wanted the title or not. "There were qoru in the assault on Karnish. I was there, and I am telling you that Jawrar has penetrated Blaze once already. And he will do it again."

"Karnish. Yes." Xane's face darkened. "I've been diplomatically ignoring that incident. But since you bring it up, tell your damn Citadel council that if they stage games on Blaze's territory again, we will consider it an act of war." Xane stopped, his eyes narrowing. "Is that what this is about? The

Citadel trying to turn Slait and Blaze against each other, to blame King Griorgi for the mess they caused in one of our border cities?"

Tye braced his hands on his armrests, fury roiling through him, but felt a cool hand on his before he could rise.

"Perhaps His Highness might question his patrols." Lera's voice of soft reason settled into the blazing air between the males. "Certainly, you've guards in the Gloom and elsewhere? If nothing else, it will keep the guards' commander on his toes to know the prince is monitoring his work."

Xane seemed to take in Lera for the first time with a growing smirk—her creamy skin and soft curves. Rising from his seat, he stepped forward and traced his finger along the girl's cheekbone, making every muscle in Tye long to break the bastard's hand for it.

Instead of biting Xane's fingers off, Lera leaned into his touch for a moment before smiling at the prince and cutting her eyes to the door. "Have you a guardsman who'd answer your call, Your Highness?"

Xane threw back his head and laughed. "A coy little thing, aren't you? Your companion would do well to take note."

Trailing a nail across Lera's collarbone, the prince strode to the door and spat out orders.

Stars, Lera was good. She may have just singlehandedly, in no more than four sentences, turned around their chances. And Tye would show her just how grateful he was later, when all this was over—something to focus his furious mind on before losing control entirely.

Moments later, a tall fair-haired male in a crisp burnt-red uniform strode into the sitting room, lowering to one knee before Xane quickly enough to conceal his look of contempt.

Xane glanced at Lera indulgently. "Leralynn, this is

Captain Mullen, who's in charge of Ferno's security. Mullen, this wee human imagines that, after centuries of quiet, an attack from no less than Mors is hovering over our heads. Please assure her that you've noted nothing unusual."

Mullen's head snapped up, his face suddenly cautious enough to make Tye tense. The male's fear filled Tye's nose.

TYE

*T*ye's eyes sharpened, the scent of the guard captain's fear eroding the last strands of patience he had for the prince.

"Are you asking me to expand on my reports, sir?" Mullen asked carefully, blanching at the flash of confusion on Xane's face. Stars, the prince had read no reports and Mullen knew it. Knew, too, who Xane would ensure got blamed for his own oversight. The captain cleared his throat. "There have been four incidents, Your Highness. An increase in sclices, piranhas, and other Mors scum—as if they have a new passageway. In light of the recent Karnish activity, I have people on alert. We've asked for additional personnel."

Lera gripped Tye's arm. "Griorgi may have opened small passages in preparation or practice for the assault. It would explain the increase in Mors rodents."

"Griorgi is working with Mors?" The captain's attention snapped to Lera and Tye, the professional assessment in his pale-blue eyes a stark contrast to Xane's absurdity.

The prince's hands tightened on his armrests, the rapid pounding of his heart visible in the soft triangle of his neck. Bloody stars, the prince wasn't being stupid—he was simply, disgustingly terrified. Having hidden his head in the sand for weeks, the coward had no notion of how to handle either danger or the truth. And if Tye remembered correctly, the only thing more frightening to Xane than Mors was his own father—who'd be furious to learn of Xane's delay.

"Your Highness," Lera said, plainly making a similar assessment. In her dress of flowing green silk, Tye's Lilac Girl was as bright and potent as a summer meadow rippling in the sun. Despite being the smallest figure in the throne room, the radiance of her personality filled the space more than the prince himself did. Crouching before Xane's chair, Lera gentled her voice. "We need to take action."

Xane nodded slowly. Rose to his feet. Paced the room. "Here is what we are going to do," he said finally, turning to face them after three rotations. "Mullen will redraft the gibberish he's been writing into a—"

"Stop." Tye's order echoed through the room, surprising him as much as Xane. His mouth dried but his chin rose nonetheless. Three centuries ago, Xane destroyed him. Tye couldn't let it happen again—to anyone. Especially not with Lera watching. Taking the two strides to the prince, Tye grabbed his tunic. Up close, Xane smelled of cinnamon perfume and the roast duck he ate for lunch—and acrid fear. "This isn't about covering up your incompetence, you little shit. This is about preventing the deaths of thousands. Maybe more. Understand?"

Xane's pale-green eyes flashed. He managed to look down his nose at Tye even with the latter holding him on tiptoes. "I understand that I'm the one who's kept your wench of a sister employed, when there are many males who'd have taken her in for other means." Xane's voice drops. "You might imagine you have some misguided threads of authority, but the reality is that the Citadel's power ends at the border. Here, Tyelor, you are at *my* command. Do exactly what I say and I will confine the punishment to you alone. Disobey and . . ." Xane smiled cruelly at Lera.

Before Tye could reply, Lera grinned, showing her teeth. "I'd like to see you try, princeling."

Xane growled, shoving Tye's chest. When that failed to do anything, the prince turned toward the captain. "Mullen, take that wench into custody. And don't be gentle about it."

Mullen's head snapped up, his body staying rigidly in place. "On what charges, sir?"

"On the order of the prince of Blaze," Xane shot back. When Mullen still hesitated, the prince's voice chilled to ice. "I understand that your son joined the guard ranks recently. I do hate to see young ones' careers end before they start, but discipline must be maintained. Don't you agree?"

Mullen shot Tye an apologetic look and rose, taking a determined step toward Lera.

Ice shot through Tye's veins and his magic surged, sparks dancing along his skin. Throwing Xane to the floor, Tye advanced on him with red-tinged fury. He had tried to be the kind of controlled male that River would have been, he truly had. He'd let Xane's taunts go unpunished, had focused on the grim reality of the situation, had urged action that went beyond their centuries-old conflict.

But no more.

"What are you going to do, Tyelor?" the prince spat, spots of red appearing high on his polished cheeks. "Attempt to kill me? How do you imagine the future unfurling after that?"

Xane snorted, a shield shimmering into place around him. "Mullen, you have your orders. And search the whore for weapons while you're at it."

"Get your hands off Leralynn," a hard voice said from the doorway behind them. A voice Tye hadn't heard in weeks. "In the name of the Citadel."

"Touch my brother and I will kill you," added another. "That's in my own name."

Turning to the door, Tye beheld his sister, her uniform still spattered with laundry soap, a set of keys dangling from her hand. Beside Saritta, Viper and his four quint brothers stood in grim formation, weapons and magic at the ready.

Xane scrambled to his feet. "The Citadel has no business in Blaze."

"Oh, my mistake," Viper said, his sharp features lit with cool humor. "We'll rip you to shreds for our own pleasure and bear the elders' punishment later." He turned to take in Tye and Lera with his turquoise gaze. "The Elders Council received Autumn's letter and has been gathering forces at the border. Klarissa is attempting to open talks with the Blaze king directly but getting no response. Word reached us that you two were here, and seeing as I owe Leralynn my life, we decided to try and be of use."

Relief washing over him, Tye left off threatening Xane to face Viper and Saritta fully. Saritta—despite having plainly led Viper's quint here—still refused to look at him. One step at a time. "This is welcome news," Tye said, meaning every word. "Blaze is utterly unprepared and will need the Citadel's help tomorrow."

"Tomorrow?" Mullen, who'd been standing uncertainly in the middle of the mess, now turned his intelligent eyes on Tye.

"Have you reason to believe something will happen tomorrow, specifically?"

"Tomorrow is Samhain," Tye said. "Not only will most of Blaze be out celebrating, but the wards between Lunos and Mors will also be thinnest then. If Griorgi hopes to open a portal large enough for a Mors army, Samhain is his best chance."

Mullen shook his head, blue eyes widening. "Sir, Blaze *celebrates* Samhain tomorrow, but that was a decision of convenience that Blaze royalty made centuries ago, to ensure the celebration falls on a rest day. Few beings pay any mind to it now, but my grandmother on my father's side—"

"When is Samhain?" Lera grabbed Tye's upper arm hard enough to bruise, her eyes boring into the captain. "When does it fall by the celestial calendar?"

Viper stepped forward, touching Lera's shoulder as he spoke softly. "The true day? It's tonight, lass."

LERA

onight. *Tonight.* My eyes stray to a window—the dimming light beyond it more frightening than any weapon—then drop, absurdly, to my clothes. A silk dress. No sword. No armor. Nothing. I pull my worries back where they belong. Even if Xane sees reason now, will there be time to get troops in place? Will River and the others still be alive hours from now, or will their utility to Griorgi have ended, snuffing out their lives?

A shiver races through me at that, silencing all thought.

Rap. Rap. Rap. The phantom sound of qoru legs tapping on stone echoes in my memory, the havoc of both Karnish and Coal's nightmares replaying on my mind's stage. *Rap. Rap. Rap.*

"Where?" My voice sounds too calm to be mine, my thoughts racing so quickly that it's an effort to slow down long enough to form words. "Where is Ferno's most populated place right now? If Griorgi does strike this evening, where would he do it? What's the beating heart of this city?"

"The Red Temple," Tye and Xane say together, exchanging rabid glares.

"It's a tribute to Blaze's fire," Xane pushes on, a growing haze in his voice that's reminiscent of Autumn's academic musing. Except the female fights with her words, while Xane seems to huddle behind them. "Its gold-tiled western-facing steps and towers catch the sunset each evening and look like they've caught on fire. Those of us with a fire affinity feel the power strongest there, likely due to the ancient magic that—"

"The main bonfire is by the Red Temple," Tye says, cutting off the prince. "That's where all the drinking and merriment will be happening even now, on what the city considers Samhain Eve." He draws his sword, baring his teeth at Xane. "Let's move, Highness. In case you might be of use."

With the approaching sunset, the streets are even busier than I remember, many revelers already starting to celebrate. Deep drums boom from dozens of fires licking the dimming sky, while fiddles strike tuning chords as if exchanging the latest gossip. The scent of smoked meats and spiced hot cider fills the air—the latter unlikely meant for children, given the intoxicating fumes.

My heart speeds in rhythm to the music, my breaths even only thanks to Coal's training. I take in the Red Temple's peak, still far from us. Too far. Masked children and rowdy youths rush about the crowded streets, seeing little on their path. Vulnerable. These children, these fae, all so unprepared for the horrors Griorgi is about to unleash.

I curse, tripping on the hem of my dress and discarded strings of red and orange flags, while Tye pushes aside a pair of boys wanting to try their wooden swords against his steel. Even with Tye leading the way and Viper's quint bringing up the rear—trapping Xane in the middle lest he should try to bolt—we can only move so fast. Only do so much to outpace the setting sun.

The crowds are shoulder to shoulder by the time we reach the temple, its steps filled with bards and priests, while a great bonfire crackles in a westside clearing. I stop, bracing my hands on my silk-covered thighs as my eyes follow the sun lowering toward the temple's peak, the gilded steps indeed blazing like flames. The drums and fiddles come together now, heralding the sunset's flaming climax.

Ta-da-da dum, dum. Ta-da-da dum. The musical march calls from all sides. *Ta-da-da dum, dum. Ta-da-da dum.*

A priest on the top step starts a countdown, his red robes glowing as the sun creeps toward the horizon. "Ten. Nine. Eight. Seven—"

The air beside the priest ripples, thickening. Gripping my attention, if not yet that of the revelers. We were right. Stars. We were right. Dread and relief seize my stomach in turn.

"Six," says a voice that is not the priest's. Not fae at all.

I grab Tye's arm, my fingers digging into his muscles as two qoru step from the Gloom to desecrate the temple's beauty. Their mottled gray skin, webbed legs, and lidless eyes send sick terror careening through me. Their mouths are open in rictus grins, sharp teeth bared hungrily.

For a second, the crowd does nothing, thinking it all but a new twist in the evening's ceremony, cheering for the high quality of the newcomers' costumes. Then reality starts to seep in, to kindle the fear. The crowd marks the priest's frozen confusion. The stalled countdown. The smell of rotten flesh carried on the wind. Murmurs turn to exclamations, which turn to a rumble of rising screams. The music finally falters when two more beings step through the thickened air—one as large   as   River,   the   other   smaller,   with   Xane's strawberry-blond hair.

A flash of a knife steals the sunset's glory as Griorgi slashes the king of Blaze's throat, sending the bleeding corpse rolling down the temple steps.

LERA

*X*ane screams.

Beside me, Tye's sword whispers free of its scabbard.

The panicked crowd around us parts like a great sea, the revelers trampling over each other in a desperate shove to get away. In no more than five heartbeats, the lane between Griorgi, standing at the top of the temple steps, the dead king bleeding at the bottom, and Xane, trembling ten paces away, is clear.

Mullen leaps toward the steps, toward his fallen king, only to be flicked aside by Griorgi's magic like a bug striking a window.

"Ironic, isn't it, Xane?" Griorgi says to the prince, now so pale he must hold on to one of Viper's quint mates just to avoid falling. "You expend such effort contriving ways to hide the truth from your sire, and now it's all for naught. Don't feel *too* humiliated though. Klarissa is still dancing along the border, negotiating with a corpse."

An unintelligible choking sound emerging from Xane's throat makes me pity him for a moment, not that it does the male any good.

Griorgi beckons the prince toward him. "Now then, colt. Let us discuss your options. Namely, would you rather spare your court pain and bloodshed by acknowledging me as your liege, or shall we accomplish the same end with the encouragement of my allies?"

The two qoru, standing at ease until now, suddenly straighten and step forward to flank the Slait king.

Everything inside me focuses, my pulse and breath steadying as the field of battle unfurls before me. If Griorgi is here, River and the others can't be far. And there are better things for us to be doing than watching the king break Xane's resolve.

I grab Viper's wrist. "Tell Klarissa to engage," I whisper into his ear, moving to Tye without waiting for a response. Whether or not Griorgi manages to pull Xane—and therefore all of Blaze—over to his side, the true turn of battle rides on the portal that the bastard must still be opening. And where there is a portal, there will be River. The others too, if Griorgi is using them as leverage. The war is coming, whether I'm dressed for it or not.

Understanding my silent question, Tye holds out a hand, mouthing, *"Gloom."*

The moment our fingers touch, I feel the pull, my body stepping through the invisible veil between the worlds of light and darkness. As the Gloom focuses around me, my hand tightens around Tye's. Even after weeks of transitions, the initial moments of entering the dimness are still disorienting. Add in the blood rushing through my ears, and for a moment, I can't work out why the pounding drums and ringing screams have suddenly cut off. Why, instead of looking up at the temple's bloodstained steps, I now stare at the inner walls of its towering nave, the rows of pews and the great altar somehow having made it into the Gloom. All of it—even the stained-glass windows, which I imagine would normally beam at this time of day—is covered with glowing blue moss.

I've never seen the like. The thick, velvety parasite is everywhere. Wrapping around pillars, hanging in uneven patches along the walls, growing so thickly around the altar that the heavy stonework is barely visible beneath the blue carpet. Thick as the moss is, it seems to be moving, the tendrils shifting in a nonexistent breeze. Feeding on the grand influx of magic filling the space.

As my eyes rove over the dim, cavernous hall from our shadowed hideout at the edge, it takes me a moment to register what I'm seeing, but then my heart leaps into my throat. Only Tye's hand on my arm keeps me from sprinting across the dull marble floor.

At the far end of the room, Shade and Coal kneel beside each other, bodies heavy with exhaustion. I see no immediate restraints, but the glazed pain in their eyes fills in the gaps—some dark power of Griorgi's keeps them and their magic caged. As do the half dozen qoru surrounding them, using blades and boots to clear moss-free patches for themselves. Wearing little beyond boots, loincloths, and sword belts, the qoru are taking no chances with the moss burning their exposed gray skin.

In the open space before the raised sanctuary and its altar, River crouches before an elaborate design painted in harsh, dark-red strokes on the stone floor. *Blood*, my mind whispers. A warped version of a seven-pointed star, about the width of a barn door, with too many dashes and swirls and carefully painted symbols for me to track. With a quick slice of his knife, River adds another gash to his already-bleeding forearm. The blood catches on his dark metal cuff before overflowing and continuing down to the floor.

My throat burns with acid and tears. Even in the perverted light of the Gloom, River looks too pale. Ill. Dark bags hang under his eyes, and his hair is matted to his forehead and temples. Such a far cry from the clean, upright commander I'm used to that I can barely believe it's him. A thin stream of blood trickles from his cut limb, that intricate seven-pointed painting soaking it up hungrily. Evil wafts from the rune, as stomach-turning as the qoru's stench. I've no notion of how River can bear to stand there, when not even the moss comes near. An island of bare stone in a blue velvet sea.

"Can you move no faster?" a familiar, deathly voice demands from an invisible place just above the rune, where the portal to Mors is brewing into existence. Jawrar.

"I could. So long as you little mind the qoru coming through in pieces," River says, his steady tone strong enough to fool most beings. But not me. Not Tye either, who releases a small, protective growl. River lifts his face, his eyes widening for a moment at the sight of us, before lowering it again quickly. "Plus, I'm not doing anything drastic until my father returns."

Just as the cool hilt of a blade touches my palm, Tye sliding me a spare sword, Jawrar and four more qoru step through thick nothingness into the nave. The emperor strides past River with an annoyed huff.

For a moment, his gleaming blood-red eyes are all I can see. Then the mottled gray skin stretching over misshapen bones. The jewel-encrusted sash, joined now by a ruby-studded sword belt that looks eerily similar to Griorgi's. The emperor's sharp teeth clack and he sniffs the air. The hair on the back of my neck rises.

"Good thing the stars sent us a snack while we wait," he says. He snaps his fingers at his accompanying henchmen, who break into a run toward Tye and me immediately, while their disciplined companions maintain their previous stations.

Tye raises a large shield around us but it's too late. I gasp as the Mors nightmares rip the protection to shreds without so much as tripping. They are used to such magics from the slaves they keep.

My males' voices rise in warning, as does my own leaping heart. Raising the sword Tye gave me, I hold the tip between me and the approaching beasts. Force myself to inhale. Judge the speed of approach, the stench that somehow grows even more pungent. Four steps. Three. One. Lunging forward just as the first of the qoru enters my range, I swing for its thin, veiny neck.

My sword slices the air, an extension of my arm after all of Coal's drills. For a moment, I think it's someone else inside my body, stepping and swinging and closing in for the kill. I'm as surprised as the qoru is when the sharp edge of my blade bites into its flesh. Hits bone.

Black liquid flows from the wound, the stench making my stomach turn. In my side vision, I see two more qoru rushing up. I yank back my sword, cursing when the blade remains stuck in the bone. My heart races, my arms heaving with all my might.

A fist jams into my gut, stopping my breath. Beside me, a trio of qoru take Tye to his knees.

I pull desperately on the sword, which finally slides free of the dead body just as a pair of gray arms clamps around my waist. The qoru's wet breath skitters over the back of my neck, the sound of its clicking teeth like nails on slate. Switching my hold on the sword, I aim the blade behind me, mapping its path in my mind's eye.

A second pair of qoru hands is on me before I can finish the blow, long gray fingers gripping my sword hand. A moment later, pain explodes in my wrist, the crack of bone and my own scream sounding too dull in the Gloom.

"Lera!" Shade's voice reaches me through the haze of pain. Before I can scream again, Shade stands, his yellow eyes flashing wildly.

"No!" River shouts.

Coal grabs for Shade and misses, his sluggish movements sending a different brand of agony through me.

Ignoring the males' warnings, Shade leaps into the air toward me and—

And slams into nothingness. The very air shimmers with a momentary blackness, slamming the male back toward Coal. Shade falls into a crumpled heap on the floor, his body arching in a horrid spasm. A trickle of blood pours from his mouth, the overgrown moss stretching toward it hungrily until Coal sweeps it back with his boot, knocking over a pew in the process.

I sob.

Jawrar inhales deeply, smacking his lipless mouth as if savoring a delicate wine, while Shade whimpers, his body shifting from wolf to male and back again, over and over.

A knife edge presses against the far edge of my throat, preparing to slice. I close my eyes, unable to watch my males lose another quint mate.

"Keep her alive," Jawrar says, a smile in his croaking voice. "Griorgi's spawn will become useless too early otherwise."

The knife lifts away.

A deep laugh that could have been River's fills the room as Griorgi steps into the Gloom with Xane. Tossing the prince onto the floor beside the altar, Griorgi watches him flop about like a fish, recoiling from the burning moss until he finally collects himself enough to rise into a kneeling position.

"I'm starting to understand the appeal of your persuasion methods, Jawrar," the king says. "Establishing a hierarchy amidst the cattle might be a messy business, but it does pay dividends."

"Yes. It does." Tearing his gaze away from Shade's suffering, Jawrar turns his attention to Griorgi. "Once we unite and you add the lesser fae and mortals into your stable, you will discover the benefits you've long been denied. Even the dumber beasts can have utility or pleasures to offer, when motivated correctly. Now, let's bring the others through and get this done."

"Of course." Striding up to the rune beside River, Griorgi slices his own wrist, using the blood to make a correction to the drawing. At once, the air above the rune turns into liquid night, stretching up slowly into a pitch-black archway that sends waves of terror through every fiber of my being.

31

LERA

The qoru holding me forces me to my knees beside Tye, another qoru's blade still at his throat. In the moment while the monsters' greedy attention fixes on the opening portal, Tye's green gaze finds mine. "Five." The single, hoarse order escaping his swollen lips sends a shiver down my spine.

"Five," River mouths.

My heart lurches as I feel the sudden surge of River's power. He may be unable to use it himself with those shackles on, but he doesn't need to. He needs to do nothing but simply let it wake, let it exist enough for my own body to respond in echo. If I dare.

Stars. The males want me to connect the quint, as I have before. Each time with disastrous results. My mouth dries, images of Karnish's collapsed buildings and the arena's cleaved ground clear in my mind. The magic has only grown more powerful since. Worse, the slight waggling of the woven magic, the most I've truly done up to now, will not be enough.

To combat Griorgi's nightmare, I'll have to wield the power fully, holding nothing back. And if I do, I will kill us all. I know it. And so do the males. I can see as much in River's apologetic gaze, his sad resignation. His eyes slide meaningfully toward the open portal, through which the first of the qoru squadrons are just starting to emerge in rows of three. Feet clicking on the marble floor, milky pink eyes wide with excitement, pointed teeth bared. It's too late to prevent the invasion, but there may yet be time to destroy us all—and the portal—before the hordes are loose. Time to save the world, just not ourselves.

"I'll shield you from debris," Tye rasps, his magic rising, growing inside my blood and roaring for destruction. "You'll walk out, Lilac Girl. But you must destroy this place before you do."

No. *No.* I can't kill them. I won't kill them.

Feeling eyes on me, I look up to find Coal's brilliant blue stare. His face is grim, his subtle nod saying he knows what's just been said. Is unsurprised. Is in bloody agreement.

Shade opens his yellow eyes for a moment, his gaze full of pain and longing. He, too, nods. Mouths a farewell.

Tears spill from my eyes as the males offer up their magic to me. I trace their faces with my gaze one last time, memorizing them. River's high cheekbones and steady gray gaze. Shade's full lips and golden skin. Coal's hard jaw and sharp, sky-blue eyes. Tye's lovely, angled features, his splash of freckles, the glint of that silver earring. The orange cord of Tye's magic stretches its claws, shooting tendrils of energy through my core. It's a force of will to open myself up fully to Tye's power, and when I do, a predator's hunger seizes my heart. My muscles tense, my breath and heart quickening with an eagerness to pounce.

The need to fight and kill grows stronger and wilder as Coal's magic untangles within me, making my blood simmer while shoving away pain to a hazed corner of my mind. If I'd thought the quint's magic unbearably powerful before, now—with the males throwing all their strength and life into the quint bond—it is cosmic.

Faster, my mind urges as the first dozen qoru fully clear the portal, the next set already on their heels. *You must move faster.*

I don't let any of my effort show on my face or in my limbs, my unsuspecting qoru guard focused eagerly on the arriving squadrons.

My eardrums ache with the pressure. My scalp tingles, thousands of tiny sparks racing beneath my skin. The phantom keening I've heard only once before sounds again. Low and dangerous. Vibrating with apocalyptic destruction.

The final cord of magic smells of earth damp from rain. Grabbing the tendril of Shade's power, I wrap it around the others, the tight bundle whipping like a great fish. Around me, the moss stretches its velvet strands, growing so quickly I can see the change before my very eyes. The glowing blue even begins shifting to violet, like Coal's eyes do in the throes of magic. Yes, the moss feels the power. Wants it. Except my mortal body doesn't give it up.

I realize I've forgotten to breathe for some time and I gasp, forcing air into my cramping lungs. The power thrashes inside me, yearning to assault its enemies. Three, six, nine, the horrors continue to march from the portal. Fifteen, eighteen. More.

"Now," River orders, as if I have any control over the power pulsing in my chest.

Yet, something inside me obeys. Power thuds through me —my own power—and chaos cedes a tiny slice of ground to control. I would smile if every piece of my heart wasn't breaking for what's about to happen. My thrashing magic winds itself up for a blow. The very air in the room grows heavy, as if riding the edge of lightning. Then, it all snaps like a whip.

Two of the marble pillars collapse at once, whole chunks of the ceiling crashing down on qoru and fae and pews alike. In the middle of the floor, a crevice similar to the one I made in the arena is already starting to open. The force of the impact knocks me back, the moss softening my fall. As promised, Tye's shield saves me from the worst of the falling debris.

Voices rise into the air, the qoru's screams carrying an otherworldly anger. Pain. Griorgi shouts something I don't bother trying to make out.

Gripping my magic, I lash the world with it again. This second burst collapses the right side of the room, bringing down a dense cluster of qoru. A piece of ceiling strikes Tye hard enough that he falls limp, the shield around me disappearing. The shield caging Coal and Shade is gone as well, the two males now sprawled many paces away from each other.

Only River is conscious still, crouching in the moss-free island in the front of the nave.

He won't survive the next clash of magic. None of us will. Ice fills my blood.

Groans and screeches of anger fill the air as qoru struggle to find their footing. I've lost track of Jawrar and Griorgi in the second blast, but I know they're out there still, rallying their offenses.

The magic inside me thrashes again, showing me the path of the final destruction with a focused, intelligent hunger. The shock wave will come from the left this time, destroying what remains of the temple's pillars. Once the supports fall, the stone ceiling will crumble, the dome's weight too great for even Jawrar's dark shields. Either here in the Gloom, or up in the Light.

I can't do it.

Yet I can't halt it either.

My gaze meets River's, his gray eyes understanding, conveying his love and strength and sorrow. The magic inside me builds to a tsunami, every bit of it on the verge of breaking through and shattering us all forever—

Every bit but a small stream of power that the blue-purple moss I lie on leeches through the gash over my fractured wrist. The magic's pressure releases slightly, the edge of its insanity softening as the moss laps it up like a cat sipping cream. For just an instant that feels like a lifetime, I watch it in wonder.

The velvet moss drinks from my echoed magic. Thirstily, yes, but not viciously.

It takes without malice. It just *is.* Like the forgiving sands beneath Tye's horizontal bar, the moss is the Gloom's great buffer, keeping the magic in check. In balance.

No wonder the moss is growing before our very eyes now —it's sprouting in response to the influx of magic that Griorgi's portal has summoned, the blue-purple strands trying to absorb the extra power and return the Gloom to balance.

My hand closes around a clump of moss, its tendrils caressing my skin. Velvet and thick as a tiger's fur. The only living thing native to the Gloom.

"You aren't a parasite at all," I whisper to the moss, the realization trickling through my blood. "You are a symbiont, aren't you?"

The moss encircles my bleeding wrist, lapping more and

more of my magic as it gains strength. With some of the power siphoned away, I can breathe again. At least for a little while. I draw a shuddering breath, a new plan settling over me. One that will let my males live.

"Brace yourself," I order River. With no time to wait for his nod, I grasp the growling dark-brown cord of his earth magic and jam its tip into the floor. The resulting quake is violent enough to knock everyone off their feet without destroying the temple, stars be thanked.

With the magic's pressure momentarily relieved, all the cords of power inside me are finally malleable. Obedient to my command.

Euphoria washes over me as the magic I've only battled and endured thus far suddenly opens an inviting hand. The uncomfortable sparks under my skin turn to a pleasurable tickle; the pressure in my ears, behind my eyes, turns to a soft, massaging warmth. The phantom keening in my ears turns into an orchestra, its glorious music already filling my soul. Awaiting my direction.

Stars. I could exist in this instant forever.

Except I can't. To get rid of the corruption that Griorgi and Jawrar brought into Lunos's Gloom, the moss needs to be allowed to do its job. But it needs to work faster. Much, much faster. Which means all the magic still growing stronger inside me must be given over to it, the Gloom's blue guardian.

Working quickly, I entwine the four cords of the males' magic together, for the first time truly braiding the strands into one mighty weave. Into a single new cord whose power is unequal to any known in Lunos.

I fumble around on the ground, wrapping my fingers around a piece of sharp marble debris.

"What are you doing?" Ten paces away, a groaning

Griorgi struggles to his knees, his dazed eyes somehow full of both hate and the same abstract curiosity I've seen in Autumn's. "I know you are behind the magic's assault. Will you give it up to attack us with a sharp stone?"

"I've worked out the one disadvantage of your immortality," I tell him, my hand tightening around the shard, bracing for what must be done. We thought I needed to gather power to triumph over Mors. In truth, I need to give it away. "Immortals can't live without magic." Twisting toward River, I raise my voice, shouting one final order to my quint commander. "Get the quint off the moss."

My words are still ringing from the walls when I plunge the stone dagger deep into my vein and slice, gifting the strongest magic in Lunos to the Gloom's soft blue sentinel. "Do what you do best, my friend," I whisper to the moss, my mind already fuzzy from blood loss. "Balance the Gloom free of Griorgi's corruption."

3 2

RIVER

*R*iver screamed as blood gushed from Leralynn's arm. Scrambling to his feet, he sprinted for her, heedless of the shackles that would yank him back. Yet it wasn't shackles that stopped him two steps into the run. It was *moss*.

Ankle high only a moment earlier, the blue parasite suddenly sprouted into a thick violet forest, a glowing, sponge-like mass towering above his head, creating a wall around his circle of stone. The strands touching River's bare hands burned with liquid fire so painful that he jerked back, panting wildly.

What the bloody stars just happened?

One moment, they'd been an instant from certain death. The two lashes of Leralynn's power had weakened the temple, the inevitable third one certain to finish it off. River knew it. So did Leralynn. River had seen as much in her eyes. Jawrar and Griorgi had known it too, the former disappearing into the Subgloom while the latter surveyed the crumbles of his promised empire with wide-eyed fury.

And it *was* crumbled. Leralynn's initial blow had cracked the floor, destroying the rune that the king had spent so much time perfecting. The portal of liquid darkness was slowly shrinking, with no more qoru entering this world. Half the monsters already here were pinned beneath fallen chunks of ceiling and pillar. Another moment and they too would have died, buried beneath the temple's dome.

River had been ready for the end. Had been ready ever since closing those Mors-forged cuffs over his own wrists. Stars knew he'd tried, had reached out with his magic just to let the cuffs crush him, to try to keep his blood from Griorgi's hands. But the king had been too intelligent for such antics, and the things he'd done to Coal and Shade to gain River's compliance . . . Yes. River had been more than ready, regretting only his inability to touch Leralynn one last time.

He had found her gaze though. Held it as she readied for the final blow . . .

And sliced open her arm instead.

River turned in a circle. The five-pace-wide space around him was bare but for the remains of the rune and the slowly shrinking portal. Beyond that, he saw nothing. His space was an island in a sea of purple.

A very unpleasant sea, judging from the screams of agony coming from within it.

Get the quint off the moss.

River gasped, understanding finally filling him. Leralynn had given up her magic to the moss, turning the small, annoying snowball of a parasite into a deadly avalanche strong enough to smother all the magic in the temple's Gloom. Magic without which none of the immortal beings could survive, much less step into the Light.

The brush of moss against River's palm had been flaming agony. With their lack of clothes and deeper, darker magic, the qoru would melt to the bone. It was brilliant. Leralynn was brilliant.

His heart pulsed with pain, remembering the gush of scarlet blood from her arm—knowing he'd never forget it as long as he lived. But there was no time for that now.

Get the quint off the moss. Get to Leralynn.

River circled again, looking for a weapon. For anything he might use to forge a path through the purple sea.

The moss to River's left shifted, a large figure clawing free of it and dropping to its knees. "River," Griorgi panted, reaching for him.

Ice crackled along River's spine. Ignoring Griorgi's outstretched hand, he ripped off the sword strapped to the king's back and used the blade's point to raise the male's face toward him. Dark-brown hair, gray eyes, a scar visible beneath red, blistered skin. What must have once been a gash along the male's shoulder was melted shut. River took it all in, waiting for the wave of hate and fury that would make this final blow so much sweeter.

All River felt was the weight of agony-filled eyes.

Bloody stars. The tip of his sword lowered.

A croak escaped Griorgi's throat. "You want to kill me, colt, but you can't, can you?" He coughed, spitting out blood. "That was always your weakness. Siding with the lame instead of the mighty."

"You are right." River let his blade clink to the stone. Waited for Griorgi's triumphant smile. And kicked the king right into the closing portal, giving the liquid darkness one last treat before the veil between Lunos and Mors shut once more. "You'll do better amongst your own kind, Father," River said into nothingness, the shackles around his wrists crumbling like bits of overdried clay.

"River!" Coal's voice. Brimming with pain. Coming from the depths of the purple sea. "River. Where are you?"

"Here." Grabbing his father's sword, River hacked a path in the direction of Coal's call.

The two met several paces later, Coal stumbling free from the singeing mass. Unslinging Shade's barely conscious body from his shoulder, Coal laid the shifter carefully on the circle of clear stone then braced his hands on his thighs, catching pain-filled breaths.

Burns covered both males' exposed skin, though Coal seemed better for wear. Like Leralynn, whose mortal body needed no magic of its own, Coal's body, too, had a different relationship with magic. The oddity that saved his life as a slave in Mors seemed to be giving him some protection against the moss's drain now. "Lera?" Coal gasped. "Tye?"

River jerked his chin at the moss, straining to hear either of their voices.

Nothing.

"Leralynn!" Coal shouted.

Sword in hand, River turned in a circle, trying to mark the spot he'd last seen the girl. With the moss taller than his head, he could see no landmarks. Bloody black-filled hell. "Tye! Leralynn!" he hollered, over and over, until finally a whimpering sound too high to be one of the qoru's croaking voices caught his ear. Heart jumping, River forged a path toward the whimper, his blade cutting into the occasional howling qoru whose melting body got in the way. Just a few steps away now. One. A savage blow and . . .

Xane slithered out of the moss, red-blond hair plastered to his burned face.

Swallowing a curse, River grabbed the back of the prince's tunic and tossed him the rest of the way to the moss-free refuge. Too long. It was taking too long. "Can either of you step back into the Light?" River demanded, his own magic too drained for that small feat.

Coal and Xane both shook their heads.

River growled and turned back to the glowing moss wall, hot panic thudding through his veins. He was just about to hack along randomly when his quint bond strained, the pain doubling him in two. Coal and Shade gasped beside him, Shade rising to one elbow, his face bloodless.

No. A frighteningly familiar sensation raced through River's veins, the darkness threatening to stop his pulse altogether. "Leralynn! Tye!" His voice grew desperate, nothing like the commander he was supposed to be. The pain in the bond grew, like one of his own limbs being torn off his body, as the invisible tether ripped. Just as it had a decade earlier, when the quint lost Kai. "Leralynn! Tye!"

The purple forest shook as if under siege, a great tiger leaping through the moss. Perhaps the animal's fur provided protection. Or else the pain of the bond's tear had overshadowed all else. Either way, when Tye's tiger rushed into the clearing to deposit Leralynn's limp form onto the stone, River's world finally shattered.

Light flashed and Tye dropped to his knees, his sobs an echo to Shade's fierce howl and Coal's soul-ripping silence. River swayed, searching in vain for movement in the girl's chest, his ears straining for a heartbeat that wouldn't come. Couldn't come.

For Leralynn was dead.

33

TYE

*L*era was dead. Tye's *mate* was dead, lying limp on the cold stone, her skin ashen from blood loss. So much blood loss that the puncture wounds Tye's tiger made dragging her tiny body here did not even bleed. In the end, it hadn't been the qoru that killed her, but rather the lass herself, sacrificing her life to let the males keep theirs.

"Lera." Salt streaked down Tye's face as he dropped to his knees beside her, his body pulsing with emptiness and agony. No. It wasn't true. It couldn't be true. Tye's tiger purred, the animal desperate to offer what comfort he could. Tye could hear the tiger now, but Lera's loss snuffed all joy from that. From life.

No. Tye had found his mate. He could not lose her. The stars could not do that.

Kneeling beside Tye, Shade laid his hand on the lass's, summoning strength from stars knew where. The silver of Shade's healing magic cocooned the girl's body. Glowed once. Faltered. Then slithered away like a sheet, the male shaking his head. A moment later, a bright light flashed and Shade's wolf curled up next to Lera's body, whimpering.

River loomed over them all, unspeaking—but not unfeeling. Tye could feel the tortured pain rolling off him in waves, see it in his wide gray eyes.

"My magic." Pushing Shade's wolf aside roughly, Coal took the shifter's place, pulling Lera toward him. The warrior was so large beside her that Tye couldn't understand how the two ever sparred. How Coal could face her on the sands, knowing how easily she could fall. Hurt herself. Die. Then he understood that it was Lera's spirit that made her seem to take up more space in life, her flashing eyes and quick laugh and stupid, ceaseless bravery.

Tilting Lera's head back, Coal locked his mouth over hers.

Tye's chest tightened in scant hope, his heart quickening. Yes. Coal. The magic that the dark warrior evoked in Lera turned inward just like his, giving her the strength and healing gifts of the immortal male. "Come, lass," Tye whispered, watching Coal's mouth cover Lera's cold lips. "Answer Coal's challenge and I'll never begrudge you a single moment you spend with this bastard. I'll even stop stealing if you want me to. Anything. Just fight."

A heartbeat passed. An eternity. More.

Coal's face lifted from Lera's, his blue eyes glistening with unshed tears. Twisting violently, the warrior slammed his fist into the stone floor hard enough to fracture bones.

Tye's throat closed, sobs he could not control choking him. When he could finally force air down his throat, the scent of lilac came with it. The moss itself smelled of it, as if paying homage. In the Gloom, where nothing smelled or tasted how it should, Leralynn's lilac scent filled the air.

His face wet, Tye stumbled to the wall of moss, pulling a

whole armful into his hands. The flaming pain it sent along his skin was welcome. Returning to Lera's side, he laid the bouquet on her chest, closing the lass's arms over the strands. "She thought it was pretty." His voice was thick, his vision blurring. "She liked it. And it . . ." He couldn't finish, his hands falling limply to his sides.

For a moment, they all looked on, silent. There was nothing more they could do.

"Your moss is wilting," Xane's voice announced from beyond Tye's world.

Rage flared through Tye's blood. Twisting around, he grabbed the cowering princeling by the neck, pulling him upright. Tye's fist cocked back. Of all the things the wee bastard had said and done, this was the last line Tye would let him cross.

Xane raised his hands, warding off the blow. "The moss absorbs magic," he croaked, speaking as quickly as Tye's grip on his neck allowed. "If it's wilting, the magic is going *somewhere*."

Tye's fist paused. "What the bloody hell are you babbling about now?"

Xane motioned to his neck, gasping when Tye released the hold. "I may not be the athlete or warrior or military strategist that Blaze bloody wants, but I do know *some* things." Stepping toward the wall of purple moss, Xane took a fortifying breath and ripped off a small clump. "Look," he said, showing it to Tye.

Tye stared at the moss. The exact same moss that it was a moment earlier, coiled strands of phosphorescent purple. "I'll kill you."

Xane shook his head. "Look at the moss you put on Lera."

Tye glanced over. River and Coal looked too, crouching

closer to Lera's body. Even Shade's wolf raised his head. The lush bouquet that Tye had laid on his Lilac Girl's chest was now dull and limp.

"The moss balances the Gloom," Xane said, throwing down the fresh moss to rub his reddened palms. "I'm immortal, so the moss takes my magic. Humans are magic neutral, so the moss ignores them. And then there's Leralynn, a weaver with the ability to manipulate magic yet who possesses none of her own. In her last moments, your mate *donated* power to the moss, and I think that formed a negative in the balance, in the form of her body . . . a colossal negative, given the amount of power in quint magic." Xane paused. "So now the moss wants to even the scales."

3 4

COAL

*C*oal had hoped Tye would snap the princeling's neck. Now, he was uncharacteristically glad for the male's restraint. Something was happening, brushing against Coal's magic. A whisper of a challenge that had not been there moments earlier. A tiny spark that fizzled to life for an instant and dimmed just as quickly.

"What did you say?" Coal demanded, unwilling to turn his gaze away from Lera's limp body, draped in bloodstained silk. "What did you say about the moss?"

"It's wilting." Xane's voice shook, the letters tripping over themselves. When Coal turned to glare at him, the prince seemed to shrink into the stone floor.

"It's *partially* wilting," River corrected, crouching beside the girl. "Look here."

Coal followed the path of River's finger. For some stars-only-known reason, the mortal had dressed for battle in a green silk gown, held up with a tight bodice that left her neck and shoulders bare. River pointed at the juncture of fabric and skin—the moss wilted only where it touched Lera directly.

"Rip her dress," Coal ordered River, and he shoved past the others to tear away a great armload of moss. His heart raced, sweat beading on his temples despite the chill. Returning to Lera, he spread the burning purple strands across her gray skin and held his breath.

Waiting. Hoping. Gasping as another spark of defiance poked his magic, another tiny prick that flared and died just as the moss withered. "More," Coal demanded, not needing to explain what he meant. Or why.

The males obeyed, hauling over armfuls of moss until Lera's whole body was buried beneath a purple blanket. The jabs of magic hit Coal often now, a new burst each time a fresh purple bouquet poured magic into her. Breath held, Coal focused on the jabs, trying like hell to grab one. To hold and caress it. Failing at that, Coal knocked his own magic against Lera's, slamming it like a bloody fist.

The magic liked that. Liked it so much that it stayed to play for a whole heartbeat before disappearing. Then three. Four.

"The moss stopped wilting." Tye's frantic voice pierced Coal's concentration. "Why isn't it wilting?"

Coal blinked. Tye was right. The moss had stopped wilting, but the magic within Lera still sparred with Coal's. Grew. Yet, as the jabs and taunts strengthened, Coal felt a difference in them. A new personality, a mischievousness now balancing out the raw, predatory fury he'd felt *before*, when the mortal had simply echoed Coal's magic. And he could feel something else too—some force was coaxing the severed quint bond back to life, knitting it along the torn joint, strand by strand, into a new weave. With it, the fist clamping Coal's heart slowly began to loosen.

Digging his hand under the moss, he groped for Lera's neck. For the tiny *bum, bum, bum* of a pulse tapping against his fingers. And he felt it.

Beside him, Tye was already clearing off Lera's face with frantic motions, breath coming hard. New tears dampened his face—tears of desperate hope. The purple moss fell away until the girl's chocolate eyes filled Coal's vision. Familiar, wonderful eyes. The same. Yet different. Coal was still staring into them, trying to work out what had just happened, when Tye's voice broke the reverent silence.

"Stars," he said. "Have you ever seen a fae female this tiny?"

Coal blinked, his gaze following Tye's until he saw it. Lera's pointed ears and elongated canines, the slight lengthening of her bones. A perfect, tiny immortal, drawing a shaking breath.

35

LERA

*S*tanding on the edge of the palace courtyard, overlooking the evening revelry and bonfires on the vast sandstone square below, I inhale the scent of fire and crackling leaves, hear the insects escaping from the flames across the stone, smell the tang of yeast from the bread rising in the kitchens. It seems all of Ferno has paraded through the streets to dance and drink and frolic here in the city center. Children smelling of dirt and sweets chase hoops and balls across the square, darting between legs and screeching in laughter. A thousand flavors explode along my palate, all from a single breath. Most of all, I inhale the musky metallic scent of the blue-eyed male stepping up behind me.

"You die again and I'll make you run hard enough to wish you were dead." Grabbing my wrists, Coal backs me into a low tree with a dense, flat crown, his hips pinning me to the bark as his mouth takes mine savagely.

Fire fills me, shooting down my spine, goading me to lift that old phantom limb of Coal's magic that's too heavy to play with just now. Despite the cold and fatigue, need flares low in my belly and one of the four new invisible cords tugs on my soul. I pull against Coal's restraints, chafing against the sharp bark, desire and fury rising when his strength defeats my own.

I bite the male's lip. Misjudge my canines. Taste blood. Where before, his scent was intriguing, now it's intoxicating. I inhale deeply, running my tongue through his mouth, claiming him as thoroughly as he claims me.

Coal growls against my mouth, deepening his intrusion, lifting one of my thighs to wrap it around his waist—

"Stop and let Lera breathe." Autumn's melodic voice wedges between us. "The healers just let her out of their clutches."

"She can breathe later," Coal says, kissing my neck, drinking me in, pulling on that invisible tether between us. One of the four new tethers I woke with last night. He huffs at Autumn. "My magic is good for her."

"Your magic *was* good for her when she was human," Autumn says. "Now, it might be simply as annoying as you are."

Was human. I trace the pointed edge of my ear as I've done so many times since last night, when everything changed. For Slait. For Blaze. For my quint. For me. Even now, surveying the palace gardens, with fires licking the night sky and children in qoru masks running about in a hunt for Samhain sweets, I still can't quite grasp the reality.

I remember dying, the soft blue-purple moss covering me with warmth and promises while my males still waged the battle against Mors. Then I was alive, the battle over, the moss a blistering predator instead of a friend.

I was alive, yes, but alive *differently*. Even in the Gloom, my senses rampaged wildly, my limbs and heart not quite knowing what to do with themselves. Plus, these new tethers. Not the quint bond—though I felt that awareness instantly as well— but something else entirely. A new, deeper connection to each of the male's souls that lives and pulses with a life of its own. A bond so profound and intimate that I still can't bring myself to speak of it aloud. To ask what it might be.

My males took turns holding me, none strong enough yet to make the trip into the Light, until Viper arrived to help. We all spent the rest of the night in the infirmary, while Klarissa's forces swept Blaze's Gloom for stragglers. By the time Autumn arrived early this evening—having left Slait Palace only a couple days behind us, after contacting the Citadel for help— little outward sign of the war remained. Except for the damaged temple, two mourning flags flying atop two palaces, and two new kings shrugging into their power.

I scan my own mind, trying to figure out if I miss my mortality, my old self. But all I find is relief, comfort. My old self isn't gone—just the body she lived in.

Autumn laces an arm through mine, pushing away a reluctantly yielding Coal. "Let's walk, Lera. You should see what sorts of mischief Blaze rolls out for Samhain. And the things they do with apples and sugar? You'll think you are flying."

Apples and sugar. "Everything is so much more potent now," I say quietly, letting Autumn pull me away from Coal toward the bonfires below. With the golden sun starting to set, the bright yellows and oranges of the buildings and the dense green crowns of the trees make the city look like a painting. "The tastes and sounds and smells. I used to just smell stew and now I can pick apart the carrots and mutton and onions and… It's like when I first entered Lunos, but more so."

"Mmm." Autumn gives me a wicked look. She's dressed as

a fire imp today, in bright autumn colors with embroidered gold flames and a woven crown of dried leaves atop her silver braids. Tiny golden bells on the braids' tips chime as we walk. Compared to her, in my simple yellow dress, hair loose down my back, I look positively drab. And now I understand why fae wear soft, natural fabrics like silk and leather—my skin feels every bump, stitch, and loose thread. I have a feeling I'll be dressing more and more like Autumn as time goes on, whether I want to or not. "And have *other* senses woken as well?" she continues. "We could ask Coal to lend a bit of his body for the good of science."

My face heats. So does the rest of me. Very low down.

Autumn snorts.

I wrap my hands around my shoulders and give her a glare. "Where is everyone?"

"They'll appear any moment. Just as soon as the wind carries the scent of your freedom to them." Autumn tips her face up to the breeze. "After the healers kicked them out of the infirmary this morning, the four set up camp in the corridor, with Shade's wolf refusing to budge for serving staff who needed to pass. So the guard kicked them out. Five times. Finally, Xane had to conjure reasons to occupy the bastards, before the whole palace staff revolted."

"Xane." My jaw tightens, fury that's more than just my own rushing through my blood.

Autumn touches my shoulder. "Xane told me what he did to Tye. He is—"

"A manipulative, cowardly, highborn bastard who little hesitates to step on anyone of convenience," I finish for Autumn.

"Quite a concise description." Dressed in a well-cut white shirt and billowing blue trousers, Xane bows to me as he approaches, the small crown atop his pale hair catching the evening light. "Pardon the interruption. I just wished to thank Leralynn for what she did for Blaze and Lunos."

I stare at Xane, saying nothing.

The prince nods his acceptance. "I'll be out of your way." He hesitates only long enough to pull a book out of his satchel and extend the leather-bound tome to Autumn. "*The Concise History of Wards and Runes from the Early Separation Period*, by Victoria Stasse, as you asked. Keep it as long as you like."

"Thank you. Except I'm not returning it to you at all." Autumn grins. "I collect author copies."

Xane frowns.

"The Blaze prince has authored some of my favorite reference texts," Autumn explains to me, happily ignoring the sudden frightened widening of Xane's eyes. "He has a whole library of interesting things concealed behind covers on military strategy and weapon making."

"Writing as Victoria?" My brows rise. "Why?"

"I'd imagined it would conceal my identity," Xane says dryly, then glares at Autumn. "I should never have left you alone in the sitting room."

"No, you really shouldn't have." Autumn's smile softens. "Why the secrecy, Xane?"

The male glances at the black mourning flag flying above the palace, his gaze filled with a mixture of resentment and shame. His answer, when it finally comes, is quiet. "When your father wants a warrior like Tyelor for a son and instead sires one who gets dizzy at the sight of blood, it's best not to bring weak pastimes to his attention. Excuse me, I see said paragon of maleness approaching and would prefer to be elsewhere."

My head still spinning from Xane's words, I turn my attention to the path below, feeling the truth of Tye's proximity. But I find the path empty. Farther down, none of the figures revealed by the flames have the large, lithe silhouette of my redheaded warrior. "Bloody liar," I mutter.

"Tye *was* over there, last I saw him." Autumn points in the same fruitless direction. "Arguing with his sister, I believe. Saritta seems to hold several strong opinions."

"Maybe—*oomph*." Wind leaves my lungs as a pair of paws hits my chest, pinning me to the cold ground. Above me, a tiger's muzzle blocks my view of the twilit sky, his rough tongue licking my neck with feline self-satisfaction. I try to squirm away from the wet, gritty welcome. "Ah. Stop it, cat."

He ignores me.

Right up until the moment a wolf's warning growl pierces the air around us and two of the mysterious new tethers inside me vibrate with tension.

The wolf growls again, the sight of his black muzzle peeled back over great, dripping canines sending a small shiver across my skin. "Shade?" I say, between the tiger's licks—which have, if anything, turned more possessive. "You are jesting, aren't you?"

Grrr. The wolf prowls closer, gray fur rippling over muscled shoulders.

Lifting his head, the tiger swipes with one giant paw, sending Shade's wolf flying to the side.

Landing in a furry gray heap, Shade yips once then rises, his yellow eyes flashing murder. Hackles raised, the wolf circles the tiger, crossing his paws in a nimble fighting step that would make Coal proud. Likely looking for a hamstring to sever.

Tye leaps off of me, meeting Shade's challenge head-on, the cat's tail swaying rhythmically in the firelight.

No. They aren't jesting. I curse, accepting Coal's offered hand and allowing the conveniently arrived warrior to pull me away from the circling predators. With my new fae body, I can smell the sharp tang of possession raging around me. Need. Dominance. Territory.

"What do we do now?" I ask Coal.

The warrior grimly picks up a large club, eyeing the two males. "Now we knock sense back into them."

"Oh, put that down before you hurt someone." A petite green-eyed female who'd be in her late forties if she were human strides up to us, nothing about her thick, practical dress explaining the source of the authority she projects. Stopping before Coal, the female puts one hand on her hip, the other gesturing for the club.

Autumn chokes on her cider, spraying the grass. Saritta, also here now, cringes. They both seem to know something I don't. I look at the female more closely.

Paying Autumn no mind, the female raises a brow, waiting for Coal to surrender his weapon.

"Their mate is here," Coal explains with impressive patience. "If—"

"If you go in fists swinging, we'll have three rumbling colts instead of two." Reaching up, the female pats Coal's cheek, pitching her voice above the fray. "Tyelor. You get over here right now or I'm coming after you." Without waiting to see whether the order is obeyed, the female turns back to Coal, her brow furrowed. "What do you mean *their* mate?"

A flash of light hits Tye's tiger in midair and the male lands in his fae form, his throat bobbing. He watches the older female desperately, as if afraid she might disappear if his gaze wanders for too long. "Mother?"

LERA

"Mother," Tye repeats, almost in wonder. The hope in his voice squeezes my heart, tugging on that cord inside me. Behind Tye, Shade is back in his fae form, stepping away. Tye swallows, taking in the female's smiling face, dark brown cloak, and sturdy shoes. "You are here."

"Of course I'm here. I live here, kitten." The female smiles, holding out her hands. "You are the one who's been racing around Lunos with your quint for three centuries."

"Kitten?" Coal echoes.

Tye shoots him a death-promising glare before closing the distance, his large arms engulfing the woman with a warmth I know so well. Firelight dances in Tye's moist eyes, his muscles trembling slightly.

The back of my throat pinches, the joy of Tye's reunion mixing with a sliver of envy. I once had a mother. I *had* to have had. Maybe, if we were ever reunited, she would hug me the same way. Except, of course, mine left me, not the other way around.

"My quint mates," Tye says, waving his hand at Coal and Shade before holding it out to me, his voice hitching. "And this . . . Mother, this is Leralynn, my mate. Lera, this is my mother, Aliaanadora."

Mate. The word Tye has spoken so many times before sounds different now. My eyes widen, those tethers and tugs I've felt ever since waking to this new, different body suddenly taking on a name. Connections not of compatible magics but of joined souls. A mating bond. That's what I feel. *Four* mating bonds.

Aliaanadora's gaze softens knowingly, as if she read my mind. A very disconcerting quality that I've heard mothers possess, even if this one isn't mine. She clears her throat, the slight crow's feet at the corners of her eyes dancing with welcome and caution. "A pleasure, Leralynn," she says, squeezing my offered hand. "However, that feisty cub there seems to feel there's some question as to whose mate you are."

"It's a little complicated—" Tye starts.

Aliaanadora holds up a hand, her other still squeezing mine. "I think I gathered that." She examines me closely, her green eyes uncannily familiar. "I want to hear it from the lass herself. After all, if what Tyelor says is true, Leralynn, you are now my daughter."

Daughter. My eyes sting. "I . . ." For a moment I want to lie, to spin a tale that conforms to what the world would want, just to hold on to the offer. But I know I can't. "Tye is my mate," I whisper. "But so are three others."

Aliaanadora blinks. "*Three* others?"

My face heats. "I think so. I've only realized what I feel just now, and I don't know whether . . ." I look over at Coal, the bob of his throat all the confirmation I need to know that he

232

feels the tug too. Inhaling, I turn back to Aliaanadora. "Yes. Tye. And Shade—"

"That's the wee lupine coward hiding in the back," Tye supplies helpfully.

I throw a glare at him. "Coal, you've met. And River—"

"Is right here." Dressed in a wine-red coat over a snowy, open-collared shirt, River towers over even the other males as he approaches and gives Tye's mother a wholly royal bow. He looks breathtakingly handsome, as fresh as if yesterday never happened. For a moment, I remember his pale skin, the deep bags under his eyes, and have to swallow back tears. River straightens. "It is an honor to meet you, mistress."

"River." Releasing my hand, Aliaanadora repeats the name as if tasting it. "So you are the final one of Tye's friends mixed up in this newly woven mating bond? I've never heard of such a thing myself, but given that you five are a quint as well, I imagine it is less awkward to have Leralynn mated to all of you rather than just one. Males get so very territorial with their mates."

"Indeed." River clears his throat, the tips of his ears coloring slightly as he tugs down an already perfectly straight jacket.

"Mother." A flash of panic lights Saritta's eyes, her fingers straying toward a scar at her temple. Grabbing the older female's arm, she pulls her closer, her voice dropping. "That is *King* River. The ruler of Slait. You can't talk to him that way."

Aliaanadora flinches, memories flitting over her face so vividly that I know exactly what haunts her. What's haunted Tye for centuries—the cruel damage of some royals' power. My heart breaks as I watch the female who called me her daughter shrink back.

"Forgive me," she says quickly, stepping away from River.

Her hand rises, filling the space between them as if her thin, aging arm might ward off the large warrior. A slight shift of weight has Aliaanadora positioning herself between River and his path to Tye and Saritta. "I meant no disrespect, Your Highness. I was only speaking as . . . I'd forgotten who I was addressing."

River is in motion before anyone can speak, closing the distance to cup Aliaanadora's elbow with a gentleness I've only rarely seen. "Wait. Please." His voice softens, his gaze oddly shy as he studies the female's face. Not a royal addressing a commoner, but a younger male inquiring of a matron. "Might you tell me what you were going to say? You were speaking as . . . who?"

Aliaanadora swallows. "As a mother." She sighs, shaking her head ruefully. "After losing a son for centuries, I'm eager to fill my supper table with more children. My new daughter's mates. Too eager to consider what I was saying."

River stares, his gray eyes glistening in the firelight for long heartbeats. "I'm the commander of Tye's quint," he says quietly, his throat bobbing. "I'm the reason he's been away for three hundred years. If you can see past that to invite me to your supper table, you can call me whatever the stars you want. And send me to chop firewood."

A corner of Aliaanadora's mouth twitches, and the palm she's been holding back from River now extends to rest on his cheek.

My own throat tightening, I step forward and wrap my arms around them both. Autumn adds her own arms a moment later, then Tye and Shade, hugging first with a tentative shyness then with full strength. Finally, only Saritta and Coal stand outside the group.

"What's wrong with you?" Tye's sister asks the dark warrior.

"I don't hug," Coal says.

"Thank the stars," she mutters. "This new family was getting entirely too sentimental."

"ALIAANADORA ISN'T TRULY EXPECTING us all to come home by eleven, is she?" I ask Tye as the four males and I find a patch of privacy in a small hillside park overlooking the celebration. Between the tree branches protecting our clearing, firelight flickers in every direction, and pounding music lifts into the night sky. Despite the darkness now fully settled and the moon a mere sliver, my new immortal eyes see the warriors beside me clearly. The night's sharp air carries the scent of burning hickory, the glittering stars whispering tales about the future where I am immortal, and River rules Slait, and Aliaanadora welcomes a rowdy bunch of unruly warriors to her dinner table, complaining about Shade's shedding.

"Oh, aye, she was." Tye cringes, though his eyes sparkle with joy. "We'll need to discuss that with her."

"I know better than to wage a war I won't win," River says, his hands settling on my shoulders, heavy and warm. A reminder that, for the first time since leaving the Gloom, the five of us are alone. River's gray gaze traps my face as firmly as his hands hold my body. "I do have a thought on how to make the most of the next couple of hours, however."

His words zing through my mating bonds, all four of them at once. My heart quickens. *Four.* And I want them all. How do I explain that? Heat rises slowly through my spine then shoots down to pool in my lower half. I press my thighs together, caught in River's gaze as surely as a mouse in a snake's. Far beyond River's broad back, Samhain fires lap at the sky, the figures around them dark, barely visible silhouettes.

River glances over his shoulder, a knowing smile on his face. "They can't see us," he whispers into my ear, his voice deepening at the very end. "But I imagine they can smell us. If not now, then certainly once we give that bond of ours something to sing about."

Wetness coats my sex, slithering into my underthings. Stars. My heart thunders, my mind racing to form words I can't manage. *Yes, I want you, River. Now. But I want you all.*

River hooks a knuckle under my chin, raising my face toward his. "Your scent says you aren't opposed to my plans. So what is it, luv?"

That word again. My bones go soft.

"Answer me," River orders, the whole of his attention cocooning me. Making nothing outside of us exist.

My mouth is dry, the tops of my ears burning. "What about . . . the others."

"What about us, cub?" Shade's velvet voice says on my right, his broad body stepping up beside River's to form a corner, adding the scent of damp earth to River's woodsy freshness.

"Aye," Tye drawls, stepping up on River's other side. Despite the chill, Tye is dressed in a vest hanging open over bare skin, and the heat of his body rolls over mine like a lover's touch. In the star-filled night, the outlines of lithe muscles speak to the predator behind the easy smile. "Do tell about the others. In as much detail as ye'd like." The words are a purr, the song-like accent deeper than usual. "Ye can start by describing me."

"Better yet," Coal says, the dark, quiet warrior stepping up behind me, closing the box of muscle. "Say nothing at all, mortal." The slight emphasis on the last word, a challenge and a claim, takes my breath.

Four. Four? *Yes,* the mating bond inside me whispers, its voice of another world. The cords shift, weaving tighter. *Together. Us. Now.*

A shudder races along my nerves, my body already throbbing with an ache low in my belly. Moisture fills my sex, soaking my underthings just from the males' presence around me. Their very scents excite and shelter me, the pine and citrus, earth fresh from rain, deep woods, and unyielding metallic musk all coalescing into a single cocoon of them. Of us.

Too much. We can't. We shouldn't. I want to. My mouth opens to protest . . . A strategic mistake, given the breath River and I now share.

His wide palm cups the back of my head, his mouth descending upon mine. Sweet for a moment, then insistent. Possessive.

The mating bond purrs its pleasure, my mouth surrendering to the demanding intrusion. Heat rushes through my blood, waking my nerves to the tantalizing possibilities.

Right up until I remember where I am. Who else is here. Watching. Smelling. Growling softly under their breath as River claims possession. My hands twitch toward River's chest, determined to push him away even as my body screams for more and my sex clenches on nothingness.

Two iron grips clamp around my wrists from behind. With no effort, Coal forces my arms back down, his muscled body stepping up to brace my back, his manhood hard against my bottom. I pull against the restraints, softly at first then with all my immortal muscle, excitement roaring right alongside indignation.

"Payback, mortal," Coal whispers very quietly into my ear, snorting his amusement at my attempt to free myself from his grasp. "I remember a certain barn and a certain post. And I am going to savor every moment of this evening."

Tye's and Shade's hands slide confidently down my body, expertly separating the hooks and laces of my dress until it pools on the ground, my bareness exposed to the air. To the males, who can do anything they wish. With Coal holding my arms, Shade's hand closes around my right breast, squeezing firmly.

I gasp from the pressure. The vulnerability of standing naked between four dressed warriors as they take command of my body sends a shiver through me. A shiver that ends right at the apex of my sex, turning it wetter still. Making it throb. *Stars.*

Tye's hand finds my mound, resting intimately against my dripping sex. As if my sensations, my body, are as much his as mine. More. The heat of my desire and their bodies crashes over me, igniting the mating bond to burn as hot as the distant bonfires. My muscles tremble, my sex pushing against Tye's hand, my mouth yielding to River's with thirsty desperation.

Tye draws a finger through my folds, touching my apex with the tiniest of brushes that brings me to my toes. The onslaught of need arches my body, my lungs closing around a whimper. I shift my weight, unable to hold still for the pressure building between my legs.

37

LERA

When River finally releases my mouth, I'm so dizzy with need that the world sways, my legs weakening. Except that the hard wall of Coal's body behind me won't let me fall. Or shift. Or do anything to escape River's sensual caresses along my breasts, his thumbs circling each darkening peak. To ease Tye's much more direct game below.

The male's cool fingers slide leisurely through my folds, up and down, forward and back, brushing the sides of my bud with each pass. The ache of longing in my sex builds impossibly, and when I try to clench my thighs together, two strong feet kick my legs apart, baring my sex to the air. Rendering me helpless to ease the relentless *stroke, stroke, flick* of Tye's experienced touch, or the zing of unfulfilled need that each of those flicks sends right down to my core.

Tye's thumb shifts to scrape across my apex, the sensation so sharp that I rise onto my toes, gasping for breath. Coal's hands tighten mercilessly, giving me no choice but to feel every moment of the night and the males it brings. He bites the side of my neck, his breath hot against my skin.

A whimper escapes my throat.

"Cub." Shade's voice pulls me toward him, his hand caressing my hair twice before tangling in it. Forcing my gaze to meet his piercing yellow eyes, which glow with predatory intent. An intent that Shade keeps in check as he brushes a gentle knuckle across my cheekbone. "Is this too much for you?"

Tye's finger slides inside me. Out. Stops.

Shade's grip on my hair tightens, sending a shiver down my scalp. "Answer me, cub. Do you want to continue?"

"I want so, so much more." My words escape in a mixture of plea and demand, a truth that I can't believe I've just voiced. The magic inside me sings, the mating bonds begging to be stroked and worked and strengthened.

Shade grins, the wolf inside him growling with intent. Pleasure. The bulge in his trousers is so full I can see it throbbing beneath the fabric.

I snap my teeth at him, the only part of my body I've any control over still.

Shade moves so quickly I don't feel the answering bite of my breast until the sting ripples from the puncture. Shade's tongue laps away the tiny pain, breath hard and warm against my skin. Taking charge of both my breasts, the shifter rolls my sensitive nipples between his fingers. Already hard from the chill, the pink points throb, the ache pooling between my opened legs.

Still in front of me, River chuckles, sliding one hand along the inside of my thigh. Higher. And higher until he reaches the entrance that Tye is so gleefully teasing. Coating his fingers in my wetness, River raises his hand and licks them one by one, holding my gaze. "You taste of female," he says. "A gorgeous taste."

Before I can reply, his mouth closes around my left nipple, Shade moving his hand aside and taking the right between his lips. I moan loudly before I can help it, my voice quickly swallowed by the sounds of festivity. Two tongues swirl around my sensitive nipples before the males suckle together, their mouths firm and hot.

My sex clenches reflexively over Tye's fingers, now moving in and out quickly enough to make my breath come faster, but not so quickly as to let me tip over into the approaching abyss. Growling in frustration, I try to force the issue, undulating my hips against Tye's hand in greedy demand.

The sharp bite of Coal's teeth on my neck makes me jump, the magic inside me rising. *My* magic, not an echo of Coal's. I buck wildly against the restraints, the pressure of magic and pleasure a self-feeding loop that's taking my breath.

The rebellion earns me twin nips from River and Shade, the sting from my breasts morphing into exquisite pleasure just as it reaches my sex. My channel tightens around Tye's fingers, my moans and the males' heavy breathing now filling the air. As a mortal, I might have held back, but it's too overwhelming now. Things that used to feel good now positively swamp my senses, my every nerve firing. I want to scream into the night and I haven't even taken one of them inside me yet.

"I like those sounds." River's low voice vibrates with danger and promise, his thumbs caressing my full nipples. When I open my mouth to curse him, he leaps atop it, plundering so deeply that I can hardly breathe when he finally sets me free. His callused thumb brushes my swollen lips. "I think I'll enjoy discovering what other sounds this new body of yours makes."

I realize Shade is naked only when River yields the ground to him. The shifter's dark hair is loose around his muscular shoulders, the fires behind him silhouetting the lithe predator that his low growls name him. The male's cock is full and hard, so large that I'd swear it was a trick of the night if I'd not laid eyes on it before. The velvet head tilts slightly to the right, a thick pearly drop already beading at the tip.

Shade's hands move behind my thighs, gripping so hard and possessively that even Coal and Tye step away. The sudden emptiness inside me is maddening, but Shade gives me no time to complain before hoisting me up and sheathing himself inside my wetness in a smooth motion. His eyes flicker and I seize his mouth with mine, inhaling his heavy breaths. The size of him stretches my channel, filling a need as deep as the mating bond itself. Wrapping my legs hungrily around Shade's waist, I dig my hands into his muscled shoulders, allowing him to lift me up and down along the great length of him.

Up, down. Up, down. The pumps stoke my arousal as Shade's cock drives into me. Faster. Harder. Until my sex is pulsing with need and wanton hunger consumes my core. The abyss of release approaches as fast as lightning, promising an explosion along my nerves. *Up-down, up*—Shade slows, trailing me maddeningly slowly along him.

"More," I demand, my breath as desperate as my aching, screaming sex.

The wicked spark in Shade's eyes says he did all this on purpose. That he was waiting for this very demand. A nod to someone behind me, and a second set of hands is suddenly on me, rubbing my sensitive skin, massaging my backside, the pine-and-citrus scent naming Tye the culprit. When Tye's roaming fingers slide along my wetness, teasing my apex even as Shade continues his powerful rhythmic strokes, I have a feeling I know what's coming and I squirm away like a captured rabbit.

Tye chuckles into my ear, his intrusive finger already circling my spread back hole, ignoring my body's protest like a predator toying with captured prey. A thrill races through me even as my reflexes roar to fight. Rolling my hips forward, I force Shade's cock deeper into me while removing Tye's target from reach.

"Be still," River commands, his gray eyes piercing mine over Shade's shoulder. The male's unyielding tone makes my stomach quiver, the heat pooling in my sex igniting to a searing fire. That the warrior can do such things to me with his voice alone is bloody unfair. His eyes narrow, making my body obey despite my mind's shouting.

My hips relax, a whimper escaping me as Tye draws them back firmly, his hard shaft pressing against the opening. Need and fear mix impossibly, my body craving the very thing that my mind doesn't want.

"Breathe, Leralynn," River instructs, as Tye's impossible size breaks through the rim, the stretch intense enough to make me gasp. He groans, holding himself still for a moment to enjoy the sensations, fingers tight on my waist.

Then he's teasing my apex, the distraction powerful enough that my channel spasms around Shade's cock, the world blinking around me. Unrelenting, Tye advances, slowly enough to let me adjust to his size but never so slowly as to be fully comfortable, his breath warm and unsteady against my neck. His quiet grunts of pleasure tickle my skin, driving me mad. Each time the male pauses, his fingers tease my throbbing apex until I can't tell where the ache ends and pleasure begins, only that they magnify each other tenfold. Make my whole body quiver with the need for release.

"Not yet," River says, his eyes still gripping mine, steady despite the slight tremors raking his muscles, his cock. Stepping closer, the commander pries my hands from Shade's shoulders and wraps my fingers around his instead.

I squeeze his hands tightly as Tye begins to thrust in tandem with Shade, working in and out in an escalating rhythm. My mind fades away, leaving only sensations. Shade's fingers digging almost painfully into my bottom, my heels into his. Tye biting and sucking my neck as he thrusts, massaging my breasts with callused palms. The dual fullness amplifies each motion, my bud throbbing with each *thrust-slip-thrust, thrust-slip-thrust* of the pulsing cocks.

The abyss whose edge I ride gapes open inside me, the mating bonds adding their own chorus to the coming fall. My hands spasm around River's as a release so strong it hurts shatters through me in waves. I scream, the aftershocks zinging from the soles of my feet to the tips of my ears. "Stars, stars, stars."

I'm still shaking when Shade lowers us to the ground, his cock still hard and throbbing inside me as he flattens onto his back, arranging me to ride atop him. *Ride?* No. I can't. Not again. Not after that. And yet—yet Shade's muscled arms and hips work me right into motion, my body rousing impossibly.

Stepping behind Tye, River kneels to take his place, waits, and thrusts into my bottom just as my body dares to relax. He groans, fingers digging into the soft flesh at my hips. The great size of him stretches me wickedly, magnifying each sensation, making this new body of mine rise, rise, rise with each powerful thrust of his cock.

Kneeling beside me, Tye's firm hands grip my breasts,

squeezing my nipples at just the right time to balance the pressure down below. The timing is so perfect, I wonder if the mating bond itself isn't directing the orchestra, keeping the beat of the thrusts and squeezes and nips. Melding us into the one that we are.

One. My eyes seek out Coal, now standing back despite the hardness bulging inside his trousers. Blond hair loose. Sculpted torso bare. Piercing blue eyes sparkling, taking in the scene, taking in *me*.

My mouth salivates for the taste of him, the feel of his wide, velvety cock filling my mouth. Inside me, the pulsing magic of the mating bond calls to connect with the warrior as much as my physical body longs for it.

"Get over here," I demand.

He cocks a brow.

Focusing all my strength on the mating bond, I yank it as hard as I can. Coal jerks, his eyes narrowing. Yet he yields, shedding his pants and standing over me to offer up his cock.

I take Coal in my mouth. He growls softly, his eyes shuddering closed. He's so hard that it has to be painful by now. I suck him deep, utterly savoring the salt and thick, throbbing flesh that I want to suck forever . . . before the implication of what we've just done registers. My heart pauses, bracing itself. With Shade and River still inside me and Tye's fingers on my breasts and Coal now filling my mouth . . .

Five.

I snake out my hand to grasp Tye's shaft, his fingers on my skin not enough, as the word *five* echoes through my soul. As the quint bond strikes down like lightning.

My breath stops, the pulsing magic holding us all together, the mating bond amplifying each touch and burst of heat in a continuous loop. Driving the pleasure higher and higher.

There is no turning back now. No separating now, even if we wanted to. Except we don't. I'm certain of that, because I can feel us all.

Coal's taste explodes in my mouth, Shade's cock finding every ridge inside me while River's shaft fills me so completely that there is room for nothing but sensation. Tye brings his lips to my ear, his seed spilling hot over my skin, his voice penetrating me as deeply as the others' cocks. "I love you, Lilac Girl."

Unable to use my voice, I search for a way to answer and find it in the very cords roaring with power inside me. Entrusting myself to the magic, I feel the response forming inside my soul and spreading through the mating bond. *I love you. All of you. Forever.*

The release we find together shatters the night, our souls holding on to each other long after we rearrange ourselves to lie on our backs, watching the stars tell tales across the sky.

The end.

Reviews are a book's lifeblood. Please support Lera's story by reviewing this book on Amazon. Just one sentence helps a lot.

AFTERWORD

Wow, what a journey. Typing "the end" at the conclusion of *Lera of Lunos* was soul wrenching. With many readers asking great questions about the future of Lera and her guys, I wanted to answer a few common ones now.

Is this really the end?

Yes. Well, no. Although this *Power of Five* story is finished, I'm not ready to say goodbye to Lera and her males. Our immortal gang will be back in 2019, but in a different format. If the Power novels were akin to feature films, in 2019 the gang will be returning for a new adventure in an episode format. Think *Buffy the Vampire Slayer* with fae. The episodes - novellas - will be released at regular intervals, each with an internal story and an over all season arc. This new series will be called *Great Falls Academy*. Although *Great Falls Academy* will take place about six months after the conclusion of *Lera or Lunos*, the stories will be independent.

Why this new episode format?

Episodes are a different way of telling a story. When logging into Netflix lately, I've found myself gravitating toward watching episode-based shows instead of choosing full-length films. Since I enjoy watching this type of media, I decided to explore it with my story telling in *Great Falls Academy*.

Can you tell us *Great Falls Academy's* premise?

Yes. To protect the human world, Lera and the quint will accept a mission to go undercover to Great Falls Academy - only to face a magical accident that makes the males truly believe themselves the Academy's human students and teachers.

How many episodes will be in the *Great Falls Academy* season? When is the release date?

As of this writing (December, 2018) I only have rough estimates. I estimate the season to be about 10 episodes and anticipate publication to start in late spring or early summer of 2019.

When will there be more news?

I'll keep everyone updated through my newsletter (https://links.alexlidell.com/News) and Facebook readers group (https://links.alexlidell.com/Lunos). You can also visit my website, www.alexlidell.com

Thank you for joining Lera and me on this adventure!
   -Alex Lidell

ALSO BY ALEX LIDELL

New Adult Fantasy Romance

POWER OF FIVE (Reverse Harem Fantasy)

POWER OF FIVE

MISTAKE OF MAGIC

TRIAL OF THREE

LERA OF LUNOS

Young Adult Fantasy Novels

TIDES

FIRST COMMAND (Prequel Novella)

AIR AND ASH

WAR AND WIND

SEA AND SAND

SCOUT

TRACING SHADOWS

UNRAVELING DARKNESS

TILDOR

THE CADET OF TILDOR

~

SIGN UP FOR NEW RELEASE NOTIFICATIONS at
https://links.alexlidell.com/News

ABOUT THE AUTHOR

Alex Lidell is an Amazon KU All Star Top 50 Author Awards winner (July, 2018). Her debut novel, THE CADET OF TILDOR (Penguin, 2013) was an Amazon Breakout Novel Awards finalist. Her Reverse Harem romances, POWER OF FIVE and MISTAKE OF MAGIC, both received Amazon KU Top 100 awards for individual titles.

Alex is an avid horseback rider, a (bad) hockey player, and an ice-cream addict. Born in Russia, Alex learned English in elementary school, where a thoughtful librarian placed a copy of Tamora Pierce's ALANNA in Alex's hands. In addition to becoming the first English book Alex read for fun, ALANNA started Alex's life long love for fantasy books. Alex lives in Washington, DC.

Join Alex's newsletter for news, bonus content and sneak peeks: https://links.alexlidell.com/News

Find out more on Alex's website: www.alexlidell.com

SIGN UP FOR NEWS AND RELEASE NOTIFICATIONS

Connect with Alex!
www.alexlidell.com
alex@alexlidell.com

Made in the USA
Middletown, DE
09 May 2019